Mortal Remains

ALSO BY MARGARET YORKE

THE OXFORD DON MYSTERIES
Book 1: Dead in the Morning
Book 2: Silent Witness
Book 3: Grave Matters
Book 4: Mortal Remains

MORTAL
Remains

MARGARET
YORKE

JOFFE BOOKS

Revised edition 2025
Joffe Books, London
www.joffebooks.com

First published by William Collins Publishers
in Great Britain in 1974

This paperback edition was first published
in Great Britain in 2025

Cover art by Dee Dee Book Covers

ISBN: 978-1-80573-407-9

*The Cretan villages of Challika and Ai Saranda
and the island of Mikronisos do not exist outside
the pages of this book. All characters are also fictitious.*

Mikros — small
Nisos — island

PART ONE:
MONDAY NIGHT AND TUESDAY MORNING

LONDON TO CRETE

I

Dr Patrick Grant was in a bad mood when he entered the departure lounge at Heathrow airport, but after five minutes, in its muted atmosphere of spurious comfort his humour improved. Though his plans had gone awry, travel always stimulated him and he was bound for a land he found captivating. Ahead were blue skies, brilliant sunshine, and the ruins of ancient civilizations; if he got bored he could always wrestle with the intricacies of the Greek language.

And he would hire a car.

He should have been in his own car now, aboard the ferry for Patras, but ten days ago his white Rover 2000, four years old and without a scratch, had been stolen from the street in Oxford where Patrick had parked it while he visited Alec Mudie, a fellow don of St. Mark's College, who was in hospital after a heart attack. Two days later the police had found the car abandoned in a wood; it had run off the road into a tree and was damaged beyond repair. There was no sign of the driver.

Patrick was upset by the loss of his car; apart from the inconvenience, he was fond of it; to him it had personality. It meant, also, a change in his immediate plans to drive across Europe and wander about Greece, an intention already affected by Alec's illness, for they were to have gone together.

He was still undecided about how to rearrange things when Alec had a second heart attack, and died. Then Patrick made up his mind and booked a flight, for at their last meeting Alec had asked him to search for a young man who had disappeared.

'Your godson? Yannis?'

Alec nodded, pale against his pillows, tubes running to him from various machines alongside.

'You know about the Greeks — how important the relationship is—'

Patrick did. Taking on this responsibility brought with it obligations as great as those of any blood relation. Alec, just down from Oxford, had been in Crete during the war.

'I've had no news of him for well over a year,' Alec said. 'He got into trouble some time ago and went to prison. Ilena — his mother — didn't say why, but it's not hard to guess with things as they are in Greece today. She hasn't answered any of my recent letters.'

'Do you know where Yannis is?'

'He was working in a laboratory near Thessalonika — he's got a science degree. But that was four years ago. I don't know what he's been doing lately. His mother lives in a village called Ai Saranda, about thirty miles from Heraklion.'

Yannis's father, Patrick remembered, had been killed during the war.

'Maybe she's moved,' he said.

'Then why hasn't she let me know? She may be ill.'

'Well, I can go to Ai Saranda and find out,' said Patrick. 'Why didn't you tell me you were worried about them when we were planning our trip?'

'I didn't want to put you off the idea of taking me, I suppose,' replied Alec. 'We meant to go to Crete anyway. I'd have sprung it on you when we got there. I wrote to tell Ilena we were coming.'

'You know I like unravelling puzzles,' Patrick said mildly. 'And if I can't speak the language of the country I'm in, it's handy to have a companion who docs. Compensates for other problems.'

The quip, as he had hoped, raised a wan smile from the sick man.

'How shall I talk to Ilena?' Patrick asked.

'She speaks a little English — not much—'

'We could ring you up,' Patrick said, inspired. 'You'll be well enough to talk to her by then. I expect there's a telephone in Ai Saranda.'

'Oh, bound to be, though it's pretty small. You find little villages all over Greece called Ai Saranda,' Alec said. 'It means the Forty Saints.' His voice trailed away and he looked exhausted. Then he roused himself. 'I've written Ilena's address down.' Feebly he pointed to his bedside locker; Patrick opened it and found an envelope there addressed to him. Later he realized the significance of this, as though Alec had feared he might never hand it over himself, for it contained a brief outline, written in a shaky version of his usual neat script, of what he had just related.

'You shouldn't have to put yourself out too much, Patrick. It should only take a day,' he said.

'I like to know of someone in a strange country,' Patrick said, pocketing the paper. 'It gives one a point of reference.'

Now Alec was dead, and what Patrick had thought of merely as a diversion had become important, for the only thing you can do for the dead is to carry out their wishes.

And so he was going to Crete.

4

II

In the departure lounge of Number Two Terminal Building the tide of travellers eddied; nervous people anxiously watched the departure signs, and the less tense sat about drinking or reading newspapers. Patrick looked at them all with interest; there were many nationalities represented. Most of the men in city suits, with brief cases, must be on prosaic business trips, but there were a good many tourists too.

Some distance away on the runway outside, there was a Boeing of Olympic Airways with the coloured concentric circles on its tail. Patrick felt a thrill at the sight of it, and was among the first passengers trooping towards the departure gate when the flight was called. The flock was halted on the way down the ramp to be searched for hidden weapons. In front of Patrick a woman shaped like a cottage loaf, flat-footed and with unruly grey hair, unpacked her huge handbag laboriously while a solemn girl inspected every object it contained.

Patrick carried a small holdall which held his shaving kit, four books, three maps, two exercise books and a Greek phrase book. He had a paperback book in one of his jacket pockets, a very small notebook in another, and an array of pens and ballpoints clipped to the inside one. All this surprised his searcher, who looked suspiciously at every item, but eventually he was allowed to proceed.

The cottage loaf lady had trouble replacing her possessions in her bulging handbag. She stopped suddenly in the middle of the corridor in front of Patrick, bringing him to a halt too, while she struggled with the clasp.

'Oh dear,' she said. 'I had it all so neatly stowed away. Still — they're quite right to be so thorough. You can't be too careful, can you?'

Patrick murmured some agreement. He did not want to become her friend for the flight, so he walked on and got into the bus. It was still light; they were due in Athens some time after eleven o'clock, and he would have a short wait there before going on to Heraklion.

'You don't know what to wear, do you?' said a voice behind him. 'It could be chilly when we land.' The speaker was the cottage loaf lady, now seated near him in the bus.

'Oh, it won't be. The heat rises up from the runway at Athens,' said another female voice. This one was deeper, and held a note of suppressed excitement.

'I hope you're right.'

'I am. You'll see,' said the second speaker confidently.

'You've been to Greece before, then?'

'Oh yes. Many times.'

'I haven't,' said the cottage loaf. Before they reached the plane she told her new friend that she was on her way to stay with her daughter whose husband worked for a company mining bauxite just outside Athens.

'You're going on holiday?' she asked the other woman.

'Yes.'

The second woman said no more. When the passengers left the bus to get into the plane Patrick saw that she was tall, with smooth white hair drawn into a chignon at the nape of her neck. She had large brown eyes and there were delicately worked beaten gold drop ear-rings in her pierced ears. She was in her early fifties, Patrick judged; he noticed as she waited calmly for her turn to leave the bus, her hands clasping a hold-all, that she wore no rings.

He followed the two women up the steps and into the plane and found that he was already in Greece. Bouzouki music played softly, a limpid-eyed girl, olive-skinned and smiling, wearing the yellow Olympic Airways uniform, stood by the doorway, and a dark young man with crisp, curling hair was in the cabin directing passengers to their seats. Patrick's was next to the window. In the business of settling into it he lost sight of the two ladies from the bus.

His bad temper had quite gone by the time the stewardesses had handed round moist, verbena-scented towels so that the travellers might wipe away the traces of fatigue before the journey started.

'*Kalispera, kiries kai kirioi,*' came the swift Greek voice over the loudspeakers.

Patrick sat back.

The magic had begun.

III

The white-haired woman had spoken the truth. As he left the
plane and walked down the steps on to the runway the warmth
of the night enfolded Patrick, and it seemed that already he
could smell the scent of thyme and pines from the surrounding
hills. How fanciful, he told himself: in fact the air here must be
full of kerosene fumes. He began to wish, as he followed the
signs for transit passengers in the Olympic Airways building,
that he had arranged to spend a night or two in Athens before
going on to Crete. In spite of the clangour of the modern city
it drew him like a magnet. But he was tired. His sister Jane had
instructed him to spend his holiday soaking up the sun; he was
to swim and walk, and keep out of trouble. He was suffering,
she told him, from too much work, too many nights spent
reading or philosophizing, and not enough fun.

'You'll turn into a stodgy old bore soon, if you forget how
to enjoy yourself,' she had warned.

Patrick had sought few pleasures outside academic argument for some time. When he was last in Athens a series of
events had begun that had brought him emotional scars, and
afterwards he had retreated within the safe walls of St. Mark's
like a tortoise into its shell.

'All right, so I'm dull,' he had said to himself, while promising aloud to remember his sister's words.

Most of the Boeing's passengers left it at Athens. Those going on to Heraklion collected their new boarding passes and went into the departure lounge; among them was the woman with the white hair. They were searched once more, decorously behind a curtain this time.

Partick sat near the vast windows and looked into the night. The huge plane they had travelled in was parked just outside. He wondered whether its crew grew bored, shuttling back and forth across Europe as if it were no more than a train journey from Oxford to Paddington. He felt sure that if he were a pilot the romance of flying over the cities of Europe would never diminish.

The white-haired woman was making a telephone call. He could see her, near the duty-free shop, where there was a bubble-type booth for public use. She spoke animatedly for some time; then, having replaced the receiver, went to the bar and bought a drink.

It seemed a good idea. Patrick followed her example, ordered an ouzo, took *Phineas Finn* from his jacket pocket and settled down to read until it was time to go.

There were about thirty passengers in the plane for the last leg of the journey, and most of them had joined the flight at Athens. The air hostess handed round glasses of fruit squash and there was a relaxed feeling in the cabin. When they touched down, theirs was the only plane Patrick could see on the runway at Heraklion. He gazed up at the wide, dark sky, so full of stars: surely they shone more brightly here than over England?

As soon as Patrick had passed through the barrier, where the travellers' names were checked against a file of what must be *personae non gratae*, he was intercepted by a tall young man with auburn hair who represented the travel firm through whom he had booked, and led to a waiting taxi. He had arranged to stay at a hotel just outside Challika, a small coastal town about an hour's drive from Heraklion. His plan was to hire a car in the morning, and from this base seek out Ilena Pavlou, visit Knossos and Phaestos, and then decide future movements. He did not favour a prolonged stay in a modern tourist hotel and thought with envy of various colleagues who were spending the vacation in Greece. One married couple was driving round the mainland, stopping where the fancy took them, as he and Alec had intended; two families were sharing a villa in Corfu. Felix Lomax was aboard the cruise liner *Persephone* lecturing to the passengers. After Alec's death and the theft of the car he had suggested that Patrick should join the ship instead of travelling alone.

Patrick suddenly felt lonely as he got into his taxi. Perhaps someone else would join him. Ahead, getting into another taxi, he saw the white-haired woman from the plane, and wondered where she was going. The few other tourists were being despatched by different couriers employed by rival agents. Patrick's young man returned, spoke to the driver, said 'Have a nice time' to Patrick, and the taxi started.

How unexpected to meet a red-haired Greek, thought Patrick as they sped along the road. He looked about him, hoping to see something of Heraklion, but the airport was outside the town and their route did not pass through it. The road, straight at first, soon began to wind about among the mountains. The driver kept switching his headlights up and then dipping them to signal their approach as they twisted and turned. A crucifix and some charms hung on the windscreen of the taxi, and a photograph of the driver's wife or girlfriend. At one point, as they went over a ravine, the driver crossed himself. A notorious black spot, Patrick wryly supposed.

He felt frustrated at being unable to communicate with the driver. Each had discovered in the friendliest manner that neither spoke the other's tongue, and that seemed to be the end of it. Patrick thought of all sorts of remarks he could make in French, German, or Italian, but he could say nothing except simple words of greeting in Greek, and it was too dark to consult his phrase book. The journey seemed interminable, spent in silence. Ahead, the lights of another car showed at intervals as they travelled along the twisting roads. What Patrick could see of the countryside was rocky and barren.

At last the road began to drop down and he saw below them the lights of a small town.

'Challika?' he asked.

'*Nai, nai,*' agreed the driver.

Not a soul was about, and the sea was like black glass as they drove along the coastal road. A few fishing boats lay at their moorings in the harbour, and there was one large yacht with riding lights at anchor further out. When they drew up outside the hotel another taxi was already parked there. Patrick's driver shepherded him inside and handed him over to a youth of about fifteen who seemed to be in charge of the hotel. At the desk, surrendering her passport, was the white-haired woman. She too had driven alone through the night.

Patrick thanked the driver with a confident '*efkaristo*' and tipped him generously, which pleased the man since his fare had been paid in advance by the travel agent. The hall of the hotel was dimly lit, and a small maid was swabbing the tiled floor with a mop; the scene was bleak, and Patrick's heart sank, but the wide smile on the face of the youth was warm enough.

'Please to follow,' he said, leading the way to the lift. 'I bring the baggages,' and he picked up their two suitcases.

Patrick stepped back to let the white-haired woman precede him.

'Thank you,' she said, and went ahead. Then she said something to the boy in Greek, at which he beamed and broke into a flood of speech. The woman laughed and answered. Patrick caught the phrase '*sigha, sigha*' which he knew meant, more or less, 'slow down please,' and indicated that the boy spoke too fast for her to follow. He looked at her with new interest.

Her room was on the second floor. The boy led her away to it, asking Patrick to wait as his was on the one above. After some time he returned and they continued upwards. Patrick by now was tired enough to have slept on the marble floor of the landing without complaint; the boy, who had, after all, to remain awake throughout the night, insisted on showing him all the glories of his apartment, with its bathroom and range of cupboards. There was a balcony, and beyond the garden could be seen the lights of the town shining on the sea. The scent of flowers rose from below, and the sound of cicadas filled the air.

'You like?' said the boy, with a sweeping gesture which embraced the whole vista around them, as if he owned it all.

Patrick did.

IV

Now that he could at last indulge it, Patrick's desire for sleep fled. A swim would be wonderful; it would relax his stiff muscles after the journey. He thought about it, as he stood on the balcony after the boy had gone. The swimming-pool was just below; he could see the shimmer of the water. However, he might astound the lad if he went out at this hour; it was, after all, almost three o'clock. Better wait till daylight.

He had a bath, hoping the gurgling pipes would disturb no one, then stood on the balcony again listening to the cicadas and inhaling the scents of the night: flowers, pine trees, and the sea. Light showed from another balcony below, where someone else must be awake; he wondered if it was the white-haired woman.

The bed was made up with only a sheet, and Patrick found even that superfluous, as he lay in the darkness with the sound of the cicadas still loud in the air. He decided that he was too tired to sleep.

He slept.

At a quarter-to-six he was wide awake. He got out of bed and went on to the balcony. Now, in the clear light, he could see mountains in the distance. The pool, surrounded by geraniums, looked inviting, but the sea would be better.

Ten minutes later, in towelling jacket and canvas shoes, Patrick padded down the marble staircase and into the hall. The lad was still on duty at the desk. He hid a yawn as Patrick appeared, and said 'Good morning.'

An open door led into the garden, and beyond stone steps went down to a terrace where there were flower beds planted with asters, dahlias and love-lies bleeding. A further flight of steps continued to the beach. Bare hills stretched on either side, dotted with olive trees. Rocks bordered the water's edge to one side of the beach, and here Patrick stopped. There was no one else to be seen. He took off his shoes, put his glasses in the pocket of his jacket, which he removed and laid neatly on the ground; then he went to the edge of the rocks and peered into the water. Without his glasses it looked blurred, but it was aquamarine blue, translucent, and deep. He dived in.

It was not cold, just chilled enough after the night to be refreshing. He swam out towards the nearby headland of rock with his easy, not very stylish crawl, then lay on his back looking at the sky as he cruised slowly along. Already Oxford seemed a world away; he would have to make an effort even to remember about Yannis in this peaceful place. He rolled over and swam parallel to the shore for a while, then lifted his head from the water. Towards the rocks he saw a blob; another swimmer had arrived. Patrick swam slowly in that direction, wondering if it was a solitary-minded person or someone who would exchange a greeting when they met.

The other swimmer was a slow mover. The head remained well down in the water, and there was no sign of action from the limbs. He was like a snorkel swimmer, lying motionless on the surface gazing into the depths.

Patrick swam closer, until even without his glasses he was sure that there was no snorkel tube. The swimmer lay unmoving, face downwards in the water, arms floating outstretched, and there was something very wrong about him, for the figure — it was a man — was fully dressed. Patrick knew before he turned him over that he was dead.

V

Swimming on his back, Patrick towed the body to the shore. There might be some life left. But when he had dragged it out on to the sand there was no doubt of its condition.

He stumbled back to where he had left his glasses, shoes and bathrobe; then, his focus restored, went quickly into the hotel. The boy had gone off duty, and a pale young man with a neat moustache was now behind the desk. Patrick hoped his English was as good as the boy's.

'Good morning, sir?' An inquiring inflection of the voice, and a smile, slightly anxious.

'There's a dead man on the beach,' said Patrick bluntly.

'Sir?' The clerk gaped at him and a blank look came into his eyes.

No doubt it did sound crazy at half-past six in the morning.

'A man is dead on the beach,' Patrick repeated distinctly.

'Dead?'

Patrick wondered for a lunatic instant if his phrase book covered this contingency. Instead, he sought aid from philology.

'*Nekros*,' he tried, and added, gesturing, 'come with me.'

The already pale clerk turned even paler. He hastened out from behind his counter. Had the Englishman gone mad? In silence they walked quickly to where the body lay.

'*Christos!*' The young man crossed himself and stared in dismay at the still figure which rested near the water's edge, the head turned to one side. Dark hair was plastered to the skull and covered the face.

'You get help. I'll stay here,' said Patrick.

The clerk looked at him desperately.

'I tell the manager,' he said.

'Yes,' agreed Patrick.

The young man dashed away and Patrick looked down at the body once more. Now, seen through his glasses, it was no longer a blurred mass. It wore dark trousers and a cream linen jacket. He stooped and moved the strands of hair away from the face. There was something familiar about those blotched and puffy features: with rising horror Patrick stared down at what he now recognized as the remains of Felix Lomax, senior member of his own college and at present supposed to be aboard the *S.S. Persephone* lecturing about ancient historical sites.

In minutes the clerk, whose brain had clicked into efficient motion, was back with a blanket and two sturdy men. They wrapped up the body and bore it away — without difficulty, for Felix was not a big man — finally bundling it into the hotel through one of the service doors. Once it was out of public view the clerk looked relieved.

'Excuse me, sir,' he said. 'The other guests.'

Patrick understood only too clearly. The sudden sight of that corpse in such surroundings was shocking indeed.

'The police come,' the clerk added. 'And the manager.' This was said with foreboding; the young man seemed more in awe of the manager than of the law.

Patrick still felt numb with the shock of recognizing Felix.

'My name is Grant. Room 340,' he said. 'I will get dressed now.' He indicated his towelling robe. 'Then I will go to the dining room. You will find me there if you want me.' Despite his attire, his habitual air of authority clung to Patrick and the clerk responded to it.

'Thank you, sir,' he said. He looked as shaken as Patrick felt.

Patrick rode alone in the lift and stepped from it in a state of unbelief: Felix Lomax, dead in Crete. It was Felix, there could be no mistake; he had recognized the cameo signet ring which Felix always wore.

What a terrible thing. His mind ranged over their last meeting at Alec Mudie's funeral only a week ago. Felix had renewed his suggestion that Patrick should join the cruise; he was flying to Venice himself the following day.

'You can't get away from people in a ship,' Patrick had said.

What on earth was Felix doing in Crete when he should have been aboard the *Persephone?*

No doubt the ship called at Heraklion, so that the passengers could visit the museum and the palace at Knossos. Felix must have seen both many times; if he were not the duty lecturer he might have decided to spend the day elsewhere on the island.

But how had he drowned? And when?

The big dining-room was almost empty when Patrick came downstairs later. It was still early, and most people probably chose to have breakfast on their balconies. He'd do so in future, though he didn't propose to spend many nights in Challika. Several waiters were talking together, their sibilant voices low but their gestures dramatic; by this time all the staff would know that a dead man had been found in the sea.

He ordered coffee and hoped the management ran to rolls, and not the limp toast, wrapped in a paper napkin, which was the normal Greek hotel breakfast.

Jane, who had been to Greece too, had advised taking his own supply of crispbread.

'Nonsense. Crusty old thing I may be, but I'm not so set in my ways yet that I can't take things as I find them,' Patrick had said.

But when the waiter returned and spread before him two individual foil-wrapped measures of instant coffee, pots of hot water and milk, pale toast and a slice of madeira cake, Patrick began to wonder if her advice was not sound after all.

'*Parakalo*,' said the waiter, with a proud smile, as if he were serving the crispest rolls in Europe. And Patrick could never wound his *philotimo*.

'*Efkaristo*,' he said. 'Thank you very much.'

At least there was plenty of jam.

VI

While he ate his languid toast, Patrick thought about Felix Lomax. He was a quiet man, sometimes moody, and at times unreasonably impatient with his pupils. He had married a large, brisk girl who had turned into a commanding woman. They had produced one meek daughter, a plain gosling who had never turned into a swan; she had married a young man of, according to Gwenda Lomax, a morose disposition, and they lived in Surbiton. Gwenda spent her energy in many voluntary activities for the good of the community; and when she became a grandmother she adopted her new role with gusto. Felix spent more and more time in college, and for some time now had gone on two Mediterranean lecture cruises each year. It was alleged that he and Gwenda seldom met except at functions both felt obliged to attend. Patrick hoped, basely, that Gwenda would not come tearing out to Crete when she heard about Felix, for he would feel obliged to look after her.

Poor old Felix. What a tragic way to end. How could such a thing have happened? Well, no doubt the police would soon discover.

In spite of the rude shock he had had, Partick was hungry after his swim. He ate up all his toast, and was just finishing his slice of cake when the pale clerk appeared, looking for him. Patrick followed him through the hall and into an office where a uniformed police officer and the hotel manager were conferring.

The manager spoke excellent English, and Inspector Manolakis spoke English too, though less fluently. Both listened attentively to Patrick's account of how he had found the body.

'Dr Lomax wasn't staying here, was he?' asked Patrick. He couldn't have been. He could only have left the cruise for the day.

The two Greeks exchanged glances.

'You know the dead man?' asked Manolakis.

'Yes,' said Patrick. 'He was a Fellow of St. Mark's College, Oxford.'

'Ah — *Oxfordi* — I have been to this fine city,' said the manager, who was a thick-set man with grey hair and many gold fillings in his teeth.

'There were papers in his pocket,' said the policeman. 'Very much wet, but good. His passport too. You, Mr Grant, are from Oxford also?'

Patrick's passport, surrendered the night before, lay on the desk. It disclosed his profession and place of birth, but not his address.

'Yes,' said Patrick. 'Dr Lomax and I are — were — members of the same college.' He asked again. 'Was he staying here?'

'No, Mr Grant. Not in this hotel. We do not yet know which one was his, but that will be moments only,' said the police officer. 'We have no news of any missing person.'

Wouldn't the captain of the *Persephone* have reported Felix's absence? He must have been missed by this time. The state of the body indicated that he had been dead for several days. Patrick decided not to mention the cruise; Felix might, for some reason, extraordinary though it seemed, have changed his plans and left the ship. Gwenda, when she heard what had happened, would soon say where he should really

20

have been. Meanwhile he would not complicate things; what mattered was how Felix had met his death. Was it an accident, or suicide?

Patrick was given permission to spend the morning as he liked, but was asked to return to the hotel for lunch. The police might need to ask more questions. This would give time for the doctor to examine the body and for enquiries to be made at the other hotels. Clearly, all would be concluded with speed and discretion.

His passport was returned to him; he would need it for cashing some traveller's cheques later to pay for the car. He wondered who would break the news about Felix to Gwenda; the police, probably, primed by some embassy official. He would not volunteer to telephone her. Before now he had found himself deeply involved in such affairs through being over-eager. This time he would remain passive.

Yet what was there to be involved with, in this instance? A sudden death by drowning was sad and hard to accept; it need not be mysterious. But there was a puzzle here, for the captain of the *Persephone* had put out no alarm for Felix after leaving Crete; if he had, Manolakis would have known about it. What had happened? Why had Felix come to Challika?

VII

As the hotel manager ushered Patrick from his office, Inspector Manolakis picked up the telephone and spoke curtly into it. He was a man of about Patrick's age, slightly built, with an aquiline nose and alert, intelligent eyes. The death of a foreigner must be a great headache for the police; it could happen so easily; one often heard of people on holiday dying of heart attacks, Manolakis had doubtless dealt with such cases before.

Patrick resolved to put the whole tragic business at the back of his mind for the moment. His original plan had been to hire a car at once, and that was what he would do. Accordingly, he set out to walk the mile or so to the town where it could be arranged.

It was already very hot. The sun beat down on the nape of his neck and his shirt stuck to him. He would have to buy some sort of hat. He'd see to it after fixing the car.

There was a choice of travel firms offering tours of Crete and other services, in offices facing the water-front. Patrick went into the first one. It was busy, and he stood at the back to wait his turn. Bright posters on the walls advertised island holidays and trips to Olympia.

22

An American tourist was having a complicated session with the clerk discussing hotels in Athens and Delphi. Some change of plan was being arranged. The American was short and slim, with crisp grey hair; he was strung about with expensive cameras and wanted to stay at the Athens Hilton. Patrick listened idly while the business was concluded.

Two French girls wanting tickets for the next coach trip to Knossos was a minor matter after that. Patrick's turn came at last and he was soon dealt with, the car would arrive in half an hour.

This was efficient; Patrick said so, at which the clerk beamed, and they parted amiably. Patrick went to cash a cheque and seek a hat while the car was delivered.

There were a number of shops along the water-front and more in streets running inland to a square with a red-tiled, white-washed church of Byzantine style. Patrick browsed around and eventually bought a light-weight straw affair of conventional shape with plenty of holes for ventilation, and then visited the bank. After all this effort he felt thirsty. There was a *kafenion* on the water-front, so he sat at a table in the shade and ordered coffee, meaning to ask for *metrio* in the manner advised by his phrase-book, but was unnerved when the waiter dashed off saying, 'Yes, sir, Nescafé, *amesos*,' leaving him no time.

Despite the reassuring *amesos* the coffee took ten minutes to arrive, but it was pleasant to sit watching the harbour. There were several fishing boats at anchor, and a large cabin cruiser was moored near some steps in the harbour wall. Patrick was close enough to read her name, painted on the stern: the *Psyche*.

The American who had been in the travel bureau was sitting at a table some distance away. He was with his wife now, a well-built woman with winged, tinted spectacles and dark hair. They were consulting a map. When he left, Patrick passed behind them; three copper bracelets adorned the woman's strong, freckled arm. Patrick heard her husband say, 'Well, honey, you'd built yourself some kind of a dream, I guess. Of course there's other folk in Crete, it's no desert island.'

Was his wife complaining about the crowds? Patrick himself was pleasantly surprised at the lack of them. There must be miles of empty hillsides and deserted beaches on the island.

He went back for the car. A small Fiat awaited him. He signed the papers and took the keys.

There were no other customers waiting for attention. Patrick asked the clerk if he had any information about the recent movements of the *S.S. Persephone*. The man knew the ship; he had even been aboard, for his firm's Heraklion office supplied the coaches that took her passengers to Knossos, but he had no details of her present itinerary. However, he would certainly find out where she was now, where she was bound for next, and when she was last in Heraklion.

VIII

Patrick did not go straight back to the hotel but drove through the little town, along the road he had traversed in the small hours of the morning. After passing through narrow streets with shops and houses on either side, it climbed steeply into the hills. Overhead, the sky was a brilliant blue marked with occasional wisps of cloud; soon the white buildings gave way to olive trees and scrub. After a while Patrick noticed a track leading off to the left; he turned down it, stopped the car and got out. Below, the sea glittered in the sunlight, but at this height there was a pronounced breeze; the air was very warm though, and he felt soothed.

He took out his maps and studied the route to Ai Saranda. To get there, one must pass near Phaestos. Perhaps he could visit the palace after his enquiries for Yannis. He would go the following day.

He walked on up the track thinking about Alec and then, inevitably, of Felix. Their deaths were saddening to him; both were only in their fifties, with years of useful scholarship ahead. Alec had been a happy man until his wife, to whom he was devoted, developed a fatal illness some years ago. This had curtailed his activities and was why he had not been to

Greece for so long. She had died the previous summer, and Patrick had begun to wonder if Alec had simply been too tired to struggle on alone.

But Felix was robust. He had no reason to pine away; Gwenda had never succeeded in crushing him, and Patrick could not imagine him harbouring suicidal tendencies; even if he had, why come to Challika to indulge them? His death must have been an accident. Had he simply been walking along the cliff top and slipped? It was high enough for such a fall to prove fatal, especially if he had struck his head on the way and entered the water already unconscious.

There was something about this idea that bothered Patrick, but he could not pin it down. Meanwhile, it was too hot to walk with much pleasure, so he went back to the car and drove into the town again. Perhaps he could buy an English paper.

This was an optimistic notion, but he learned that they would arrive in the early evening. He returned to the *kafenion* by the water-front and ordered a beer. While he sat there a caique came in filled with passengers who had been to one of the tiny off-shore islands where there were some traces of very early civilization. The tourists trooped on to the jetty looking hot.

A slight, dark girl went past the tables. She wore a white shirt and a yellow skirt, and her legs were tanned.

He shouldn't be here alone; that was the trouble.

He watched her out of sight. Funny how he always noticed slight, dark girls. He should react to blondes; he might have better luck.

As he drove back to the hotel he saw a woman in a blue dress trudging along. A silk scarf was tied round her head and she wore dark glasses. It was Patrick's white-haired travelling companion of the night before. He stopped and offered her a lift.

'Thank you,' she said, getting in beside him. 'It's very hot walking.'

'It was a tiring journey last night,' said Patrick.

'I suppose it was. I never sleep much the first night anyway. Over-excitement, I expect. But in this heat I collapse every afternoon.'

'You've been to Crete before?'

'No, never. But to several islands and various parts of the mainland. I know Athens well.'

'That's where you learned Greek?'

'No. I made a serious effort at home, since one feels so inadequate being unable to communicate,' she said. 'But it's a difficult language. So many syllables. You don't speak it?'

'No.'

'You had a dreadful experience this morning, I understand. The waiter who brought my breakfast up told me. They've been ordered not to discuss it, because of upsetting the visitors, but when I spoke to him in Greek, out it all came. He'd seen the body in some inner fastness of the hotel. It must have been a shock — he was only about fourteen. "The new English *Kirios* found him," he said. That could only be you.' She did not tell Patrick that she, too, had woken early and had seen him walk down to the beach. 'Was it someone from the hotel?'

'No. They don't know where he was staying,' Patrick said. 'But he was a colleague of mine. A friend.'

'Oh no! How awful! What a terrible thing!'

Patrick recognized that he was suffering badly from a lack of human contact; he needed to talk.

'Are you in a hurry, or shall we go past the hotel and see what lies round the headland?' he asked her.

'Let's do that,' she agreed at once.

The road wound on past their hotel parallel to the shore; on either side pines and olive trees sprouted from the dry soil, and there were occasional fields of carob bushes now being harvested. A woman dressed in black worked in one, her donkey standing beneath a tree. Some chickens scratched nearby. Soon they reached a stretch where there was room to park off the road in the shade of an olive. Far in the distance, across the gulf, high arid mountains, grey and tipped with wisps of cloud, met the wide sky. They got out of the car and stood under the tree, looking at the view.

'Africa's over there. Imagine it,' said Patrick. 'One forgets how close it is.'

The sea beyond them was whipped up now into little waves, and a strong, very warm breeze blew around them.

'Look at the sea. This is the hot wind from the desert,' said Patrick's companion.

'The sirocco.'

'Yes. Tell me about your poor friend.'

'Yes — well, let me introduce myself first. My name's Grant, Patrick Grant. I'm a university lecturer.'

'And mine's Ursula Norris. I'm an art historian,' said the woman. She took off her dark glasses and regarded him steadily. Evidently she approved of what she saw, for she smiled warmly. Patrick smiled back. Then he told Miss Norris about Felix, but he did not mention the cruise.

'I suppose he slipped while walking on the cliff. It looks a pleasant stroll along the promontory, but if one lost one's footing—? There's very little tide, to wash him in from further off,' she said.

Suddenly Patrick realized what had bothered him earlier about this idea. Into his mind sprang the image of Felix, green-faced, hastily leaving the roof of St. Mark's where they were both, as members of the same committee, inspecting the lead covering.

'I can't believe it happened like that,' he said. 'Felix suffered from vertigo. He'd never walk willingly near the edge of a cliff.'

'Some boat, then? A dinghy? He might have hired one.'

'It must have been something of the sort, I suppose.' But if a tourist in a small boat didn't come back, someone would look for him, surely? And Manolakis said no one was missing. 'But if so, what on earth was he up to, out in a small boat alone wearing flannels and a jacket, and his Vincent's tie?' said Patrick.

'Was he dressed like that?'

'Yes.'

Ursula was silent.

'Was he married?' she asked at last.

'Yes, but his wife never went away with him. She's quite a tough nut,' said Patrick.

'She's in for a shock,' said Ursula.

'She'll bear it.' Patrick could imagine Gwenda in her role as a widow.

'People do act out of character sometimes,' said Ursula slowly.

'You mean Gwenda Lomax may mourn?'

'She may — but no. I was thinking there may be some reason for your friend's landlubberly attire aboard a small boat.'

'I wish I knew what it was,' said Patrick.

'The police will probably have some theory or other by now,' said Ursula.

Patrick hoped she was right. As they drove back to the hotel he discovered that she was staying in Crete for only a week. Then she was going to Athens.

'I come out every year,' she said. 'This time I'm staying indefinitely.' She did not explain any more.

When they reached the hotel Inspector Manolakis's car and driver were waiting outside, and the manager was looking for Patrick.

IX

The authorities had accomplished a good deal during the morning. Felix's death had been caused by drowning; there were
contusions on the body consistent with a fall from the cliffs,
including a bruise on the back of the head. He had had a good
deal to drink before death: ouzo, it seemed. The assumption was
that, under the influence of excess alcohol, he had lost his footing and fallen into the sea. He had been dead about four days.

'In this heat, Mr Grant, you understand me, the body
would rise to the surface quickly,' said Manolakis. He sat at
the manager's desk, his clever eyes watching Patrick's response.

Patrick nodded. He was satisfied that Felix had drowned;
he had noticed a little froth issuing from the dead man's nos-
trils before he was bundled into his blanket, after that dreadful
moment of recognition.

'He is to be sent home for burial,' added the policeman
with evident relief. 'It is the wish of the widow.'

She would stage a tragic funeral. Well, at least Patrick
need not attend.

'Was he staying on the island?' he asked.

'Ah — that is the puzzle. We find no record, and he was
not reported missing. It is very strange.'

'He didn't come over for the day and go out in a small boat—? No.' Patrick saw Manolakis's expression.

'No small boat is lost,' said Manolakis.

It was quite impossible for Felix to have vanished from the *Persephone* without a hue and cry being raised; therefore his absence from the ship had been explained. Ursula had said that people acted out of character at times; so they did, but not balanced men like Felix. Yet there were his moods, the times when he was silent, brooding. And he was only a moderate drinker; why was he full of ouzo? To beat the vertigo? Why not avoid the cliff?

Would this satisfy Gwenda, or would she demand further enquiries? Would she even care enough to wonder?

'You are not happy, Mr Grant,' said Manolakis. 'There are lonely men who give no reason for their actions and are not missed swiftly.'

So Manolakis thought that Felix had jumped.

'An accident. It is better so,' added the policeman. 'There is no evidence to prove otherwise.'

That was true, anyway. Felix's thoughts in his last hours would never be known, it seemed. It was tragic, but there was nothing more to be said. Patrick himself was to be let off lightly; arrangements were already in hand for flying the body home as soon as the official enquiry was over, and he could put the whole thing out of his mind and concentrate on Yannis.

He took *Phineas Finn* in to lunch with him and scarcely lifted his eyes from its pages while he plodded through a hefty *moussaka*. Afterwards he went up to his room. The shutters were drawn but the room was still warm. He played about with the air-conditioning; opening the window presumably defeated the whole object of it, but one could not shut out this glorious day. He flung the windows wide.

It was too hot to sit out for long, even in the shade.

Ursula Norris was doubtless having her siesta. It wasn't a bad idea.

Patrick lay down on his bed and immediately the image of a slight, dark girl floated into his mind.

It was ridiculous. He'd got over it months ago. It was just the effect of this place — the sun and the surroundings, and the sight of at least four honeymoon couples in the hotel restaurant.

It was better to think about Felix.

X

Patrick slept for an hour, and woke feeling heavy-headed.

He put slacks and a shirt on over his swimming trunks and went outside.

The hotel beach was strewn with toasting bodies. Some slept, some read; a few heads bobbed in the sea. A fat middle-aged woman spread oil on the back of her still fatter husband. A few people glanced up as Patrick passed. He felt a sharp revulsion from so much naked flesh and walked on towards the promontory below which Felix's body had been floating.

On the cliff top there were patches of shrivelled grass and scrub. He was no botanist, but he knew that these withered bushes must be bright with blossom in the spring. Close to the sea's edge the ground was bare, just grey rock above the water. At the tip of the small peninsular there was an old wartime pillbox set into the rock. It was easy to imagine sentries inside it, watching for the submarines that brought supplies to the *andartes*. Patrick wondered why it had not been demolished. It was still a solid structure. Perhaps it served as a warning. More likely it was a refuge for local lovers, since the present chaste regime forbade public display. There were some cigarette ends on the ground inside it, and various *graffiti* scratched on the stones of the inner walls, but nothing of interest. Patrick strolled slowly on, and soon, seeing a flat rock beneath him, climbed down to it. It made a secluded retreat, so he stripped to his trunks and stretched out there for a while, reading. When he grew too hot he dived off the rocks into the deep, clear water, and swam for a long time.

He dried out in the sun, and then went back to the hotel. The evening yawned ahead, full of empty hours. He would invite Ursula Norris to join him for a drink.

But when he came down later to the terrace bar she was with an elderly couple and did not seem to notice him. Patrick, sulking slightly, ordered an ouzo, and sat with his back to her, facing an enormous *amphora* which was securely cemented into the flower bed among the geraniums. One of the honeymoon couples appeared, each partner totally absorbed in the other; they looked about eighteen years old. Patrick felt old and bitter. There were three girls chattering together at another table. They glanced at him, then very obviously began to discuss him; one girl stared at him boldly. Patrick turned away from them and opened his book.

Once he'd started his programme he'd be all right. An expedition to somewhere of interest each day, that was the thing, and enquiries about Yannis; then he would leave Crete. In Athens there was plenty to do; he had met people at the Embassy when he was there before and might renew contact with them. And he wanted to explore the Pelponnese.

He decided to go down to the town for dinner. It would be more amusing than the hotel restaurant, where there were only the other guests to watch. Hotel life was not for him.

He had a second ouzo, which made him feel better, then drove down to Challika. The lights were coming on now: darkness swept down suddenly out here; there was no twilight. He parked the car and went to the paper shop. Today's *Times* had arrived. Tomorrow's might carry a paragraph about Felix; he would surely merit a few lines. He tucked the paper under his arm and went for a stroll.

The little town, which had seemed half-asleep earlier, had come alive. People wandered about the streets; the shops and harbour were brightly lit; tourists examined embroidered fabrics, jewellery, woven bags, and other attractions. Patrick saw a flight of steps leading steeply away from the water-front between the houses that faced it, and climbed them. A dark-eyed child clasping a scrawny cat watched him go by with a solemn gaze. Patrick smiled rather self-consciously and said, '*kalispera*.' The child stared back at him, silent. A youth in jeans and a striped singlet came out of a doorway ahead of him, sandals flapping on the dusty path. A long-haired couple, dressed alike in frayed cotton shirts and trousers, the man carrying a sleeping baby, went past arguing in English about where to eat.

Some embroidered carpets hanging outside a small shop caught his eye. The colours were soft and glowed in the lamp-light. Jane would like one, but it would be bulky to take home. If only he'd got his own car.

He went into the shop, which bore the name *Aphrodite*, spelled out in Greek characters, over its doorway. Displayed within, besides more carpets, were jewellery and crochet-work. A girl of about seventeen sat by the counter crocheting some garment. Patrick's *kalispera* achieved better results here, and she answered with a warm smile. Her eyes were huge in her sallow face, and she had short, curly dark hair.

'You speak English?' Patrick asked.

'Yes. A little,' answered the girl. Her crochet-hook never stopped moving.

Patrick saw a row of dresses, waistcoats and hand-knitted sweaters hanging at one side of the shop.

'Do you make all these yourself?' he asked incredulously.

'Yes. And my mother.'

In the back of the shop Patrick now saw a grey-haired woman, knitting busily but watching him closely. He smiled at her and repeated his greeting. The woman smiled back and murmured some phrase Patrick did not understand; she bowed with a regal grace. Her face was lined and her body, in the usual black, was shapeless as she sat there, ceaselessly working. She might well be not much over forty, Patrick thought, but she looked about sixty. All winter she and the girl must knit and sew to stock their shop, he supposed. He would have to buy something.

He told the girl he wanted a present for his sister. She put her work down and came to help him. They looked through the crocheted garments. The waistcoats were rather nice. Patrick asked the girl to put one on so that he could see how it looked. She obeyed, and stood before him quite without coquetry, for her work to be appraised.

'My sister is bigger than you,' said Partick.

The girl showed him one of a different pattern in a larger size. It looked all right to Patrick, and if Jane didn't like it she could give it away. He bought it; it was surprisingly cheap. Before wrapping it up the girl and her mother conferred together, measuring it and noting down details of the pattern. At Patrick's interested query the girl explained, 'Now I make another the same.'

'How long will it take?'

'Four days.'

As she tied up the parcel he enquired if her name was Aphrodite, like the shop, and she said no, she was called Sophia. He wished he could talk to her mother. Her face was calm as she knitted placidly on. He must tell Ursula Norris about this shop; she would like it. It lacked the sophistication of the more expensive establishments nearer the harbour.

Yannis's mother, Ilena, must be like this woman, so patiently sitting here all day. But she would be older; Yannis was over thirty now.

He felt cheered by this encounter and walked back to the centre of the town with a lighter step. Many of the tables outside the *tavernas* and the *kafenia* were occupied now. The babble of voices was muted by the open air. The breeze had dropped and the sea was still. Patrick reached a *taverna* on the quay which he had noticed earlier, and found a table by the water's edge where he could look at the boats moored below. He asked for mullet.

There was none. The boats had brought no mullet in today.

The waiter, apologetic, offered sardines and said they were very good.

Patrick kept calm. Greek sardines could hardly be identical with those at home found in tins. He agreed to try them, with *avrolemono* soup first, salad, and a bottle of Demestica.

'You are English, sir?' the waiter said.

'Yes.'

The waiter looked pleased, and made a ceremony of setting the table and polishing the wine glass. Patrick understood the subtlety of this when he heard a couple at another table give their order in English and then begin talking German together.

His soup came, and a crisp roll. Why crisp rolls now and none at breakfast? Yet what did it matter. He looked around him; everyone seemed content, even the waiters, though some frowned deeply with concentration as they served the various dishes. The warm air was like a balm; for the first time for weeks Patrick's nerves felt eased. Why fret? It achieved nothing. The tortoise often got as good results as any hare, with far less personal strain. He had laid his book on the table, but he did not open it.

The wine was light and pleasant. As he topped up his glass someone sat down at the next table. It was the elderly American whom he had noticed earlier in the travel bureau and again with his wife outside the *kafenion*. He saw Patrick and nodded, somewhat curtly. Then his gaze fell on Patrick's book.

'Ah — English?' he said.

'Yes.'

'Uh — huh. I'm from New Jersey.'

The waiter came to take the American's order, and Patrick was astonished to hear it given in Greek. Quite an exchange then took place, the waiter all smiles. When he had gone the man from New Jersey said, 'My name's George Loukas. My father was Greek. All my life I've promised myself that I'd come home and now I've done it. It's a wonderful experience. A man doesn't always realize his life's ambition.'

Very rarely, Patrick thought.

'I've just retired,' George Loukas continued. 'I've waited years for this trip. It was no good coming just on a three weeks' vacation. We have to see everything. We're going on to your London in the fall.'

'You're doing Europe, are you?'

'Some. We've been to Paris, Rome and Venice,' said Loukas.

Patrick wondered why he had spoken no Greek in the travel office that morning. Perhaps at such times it was better to stress one's American aspect, to be recognized as a free spender.

'My wife's not well, that's the pity of it,' Loukas gloomed now. 'She's not been herself since we got to Crete last week. The food, I guess. She has to watch her diet.'

'I'm sorry,' said Patrick politely.

His sardines came. They looked like whitebait and tasted very similar. They were excellent, and so was the salad, liberally garnished with cheese and olives.

'Did your father come from Crete?' Patrick asked Loukas.

'He did, originally, but he went across to the mainland as a child. He grew up near Nauplia. I haven't been there yet — that's to come. Have you been to Nauplia?'

Patrick had not.

The American's soup arrived. He too was having *avrolemono*.

'Do you like Greek food?' he asked.

'Well—' Patrick began guardedly. 'It varies,' he said. 'This fish is very good.'

'They serve everything lukewarm at our hotel,' confided Loukas. 'Makes Elsie mad. Where are you staying?'

Patrick told him. He and his wife were staying at the Apollo, a hotel nearer the town. He said there were representatives from every nation staying there, a number of Swedes and Danes in particular.

'I guess their own countries are just so damned cold they need to soak up the sun,' he said.

A boat was chugging gently into the harbour; the soft putter of its engine came drifting towards them across the water. It was a cabin cruiser; Patrick recognized it as the *Psyche*, the vessel he had noticed tied up near the quay-side that morning. As he watched, it nosed gently in and picked up the same mooring. Some minutes later two dark young men and a blonde girl disembarked from it and walked off towards the town.

'Kids have a great time these days,' said Loukas. 'That girl's no Greek.' He shook his head, but tolerantly. 'Still, I guess if you have everything all at once you don't always appreciate it.' He looked across at Patrick, still munching tiny fish. 'Of course, you're a young man yet,' he added. 'You wouldn't know.'

'I'm not as young as all that,' Patrick protested. Some of his pupils thought he verged on senility.

'You remember the war, anyway.'

'Certainly,' said Patrick with asperity. And afterwards he had done National Service, serving with the army in Germany and emerging with a good knowledge of the language that he had found useful many times since. 'Were you in the army?'

'No, sir. I'd flat feet, would you believe it? I went for the navy, but no joy. So I went into a factory and in the end I got to own it. I made shoes.'

'Success story,' Patrick said. 'And ironic. Which part of Crete did your father come from?'

'Further west. It was a village that suffered a lot in the war,' said Loukas. 'Most of the men were shot. I'd hoped I might find some kin there.'

'You've been to it?'

'Yes. All my folks were in the cemetery.'

Two old men wearing the traditional baggy trousers and high brown boots walked past. Their hair was grizzled and their faces crinkled with lines.

'Those two could tell you a few things, I imagine,' said Patrick.

'My wife's first husband was killed in Crete early in the war,' the other man confided. 'She's English. I guess it's been too much for her, coming here. I thought she'd appreciate it — a kind of sentimental pilgrimage. I didn't tell her I'd booked in here after Italy — kept it as a surprise. But she's soft-hearted. She'll be all right when we get to Athens. We're off there on Thursday. Look us up at the Hilton if you're in town.'

Patrick promised he would, and invited Loukas to call on him at St. Mark's if he were ever in Oxford.

There was no *baclava*. Patrick made do with the ubiquitous cream caramel.

As he walked back to collect the Fiat he saw Inspector Manolakis drive away from the police station in his large, official car. The man certainly worked late.

PART TWO:
WEDNESDAY AND THURSDAY

CRETE

I

Early the next morning Patrick set off for Ai Saranda. As he left, he saw a group of people outside the hotel entrance waiting for the tourist buses that would collect them for their day's excursions. They were hung about with cameras and string bags. New arrivals were shrimp pink or lobster red, according to their degree of exposure to the sun; a few were deeply bronzed. Apart from the group, looking elegant and pale, stood Ursula Norris.

Patrick greeted her and asked where she was going.

'It's Phaestos today,' she said. 'Knossos on Thursdays. The tour companies do certain trips on certain days.'

'I may see you there,' said Patrick. 'I'm going to look up someone for a friend of mine near there.'

'I'll look out for you,' said Ursula.

Further along the road, another group of tourists waited outside the Apollo hotel. Patrick saw George and Elsie among them. In Challika, he stopped at the travel agent's office to see if the clerk had been able to discover the movements of the *Persephone*.

An atmosphere of controlled panic prevailed here. Several people were trying to buy last-minute tickets for the day's excursions and some refused to accept that there were no vacancies on certain tours. Others had different problems. All craved instant attention. Patrick decided to wait till the coaches had gone before adding to the confusion. He walked across the road and looked at the boats in the harbour, wondering if there was much illicit trading. Any strange craft would soon be noticed, he supposed. The *Psyche* was still at her mooring. One of the young men was on the deck, doing something to a length of rope, splicing it, perhaps. As he watched, the girl walked along the quay towards the boat. Her long, curly blonde hair was secured in a pony-tail; she wore brief cotton shorts, and her legs were tanned to a rich golden shade. Patrick moved nearer and saw her go lightly down the steps and aboard the boat. The boy looked up from what he was doing and spoke to her, but continued with his task.

'Good morning,' Patrick called down to them. 'Lovely day.'

'Yes,' answered the girl. She shaded her eyes from the sun to inspect the speaker. All she could see was a bulky shape against the brilliant light.

'Are you going out today?'

'Yes. We're taking some tourists round the islands.'

'Oh — you hire your boat out, do you?'

'Yes. By the day, or half-day. Whatever you like. It's Spiro's boat — this is Spiro,' she introduced the young man. 'I'm just helping for the season.'

She had a transatlantic accent.

'What part of Canada do you come from?' asked Patrick.

'Well now — so you didn't take me for an American,' the girl said, laughing.

Patrick seldom made that mistake.

'You don't sound a bit American,' he told her truthfully, and went down the steps to see her more clearly. She was a sturdy girl, golden brown all over, it appeared, now that he saw her better. Very blue eyes grinned in a friendly way; her nose was sprinkled with freckles.

'I'm from Montreal,' she said. 'I'm Jill McLeod.'

Patrick soon learned that she had been in Europe for six months, bumming around, as she put it. Since reaching Crete she had not wanted to move on. Patrick wondered what her parents imagined her to be doing. She certainly looked happy and healthy with her Greek young man, and was probably learning the language in the most intimate way.

'I'd like to come out with you one day,' he said.

'That'd be great. You can always find us here about this time, or in the evening. We go to Zito's most nights around nine,' she said.

Spiro had not contributed to this conversation, though he had listened to them, smiling, while he worked on his rope. Perhaps his English was not fluent. Patrick said goodbye to them both and went back to the travel office. The bus for Phaestos was just leaving; he saw Ursula Norris gazing from one of the windows. They waved to one another with enthusiasm: two acquaintances amid a sea of strangers.

Patrick felt quite brisk as he stepped into the office, which was now miraculously cleared. The clerk remembered him at once, and produced a sheet of paper on which was written the itinerary of the *Persephone* throughout her current cruise. She was in the Black Sea, and was not due back in Greece until Monday of the next week, when she would call at Itea for Delphi. Then she was due to sail straight for Syracuse. She had not called at Heraklion for over a month.

II

The village of Ai Saranda, when Patrick reached it after a long drive over mountain roads that twisted and turned, and then across a fertile plain planted with vines, was beginning to expand. In addition to the original old whitewashed cottages there were several square new concrete houses with flat roofs, and a grocer's shop which displayed detergents in the window.

In the centre of the cluster of buildings a huge eucalyptus tree cast a shade under which were arranged some tables and chairs, and across the road was the *kafenion* which owned them. Patrick parked further up the road and walked back towards the *kafenion*. He took a seat at one of the rickety tables. A few old men, some in baggy trousers and all wearing boots, were already sitting at another table. They looked at Patrick curiously. He said '*kalimera*' and felt rage at being rendered inarticulate.

A middle-aged man wearing an apron came out to attend to him.

'Ouzo, *parakalo*,' he said, and asked the other if he spoke English.

'Two — three words,' said the Greek, with a shrug.

'*Ime Anglos. Den katalaveno Ellinika*,' recited Patrick in a carefully learned phrase.

'Ah — Eengleesh — how are you?' said the Greek, smiling warmly. He shook Patrick's hand with vigour. '*Anglos*,' he told his other customers.

It seemed to be a magic word. The older men all started smiling, and one levered himself to his feet, came across, and announced that he spoke English very good.

Patrick, who had begun to wish that he had asked Ursula Norris to accompany him on this mission as interpreter, took fresh heart. Someone would be able to find Ilena for him.

'What is your town in England?' he was asked, and there were cries of '*nai, nai*,' over *Oxfordi*.

He was mercilessly cross-examined.

'You are married?'

'No.'

'Why not? Ah — you have a sister — *po, po, po*,' Much head-shaking, and commiserating murmurs all round.

'Yes, I have a sister.' Patrick was puzzled, and then light dawned. They would be expecting him to look about for a husband for Jane before finding a wife for himself, in the Greek fashion.

'She is married — two children. Yes, she has a son,' he told them.

This went on for some time. When they had dragged out of him every detail of his family circumstances he felt it was time to make an effort of his own.

'A friend of mine was in Crete during the war. Alec Mudie. He came to Ai Saranda. Do you remember him?'

Yes, of course — they all remembered Alexis. So strong, he had been, so brave, so gay. He had been back to visit them several times since then, but not for some years now. How was he?

At the news of his death all fell silent. Patrick explained about Alec's wife and her long illness and that this was the reason he had not come. He spoke simply, for Petros, his translator, clearly had linguistic limitations. It all took time, and much ouzo was consumed during the discussion.

At last Patrick asked to be directed to Ilena Pavlou's house. At this there was sudden silence.

'She has gone away,' said Petros at last.

Patrick looked round the group. No one met his eye.

'Where to? She is not dead?'

No, she was not dead. But no one wanted to say where she was. Perhaps they did not know. Well, what about Yannis?

'Ah — Yannis. That one.' Heads were shaken. He had been a headstrong, ambitious youth, Patrick was told.

These were valiant old men. If Yannis had rebelled against the current regime they would not disapprove; Alec had implied that this was what must have happened.

'Yannis had been in prison?' Patrick tried. Perhaps he could force them into disclosing something.

There was a silence. Pride was involved. A mutter of '*po, po, po,*' came from one man, then Patrick heard '*nai, nai.*' He found it hard to remember that this meant 'yes' in Greek, since it sounded so negative.

A short staccato conference took place, and finally Petros spoke.

'*Kirie* Grant, we tell you what we know. Yannis is coming here one year ago. He is very—' Petros searched for the word he wanted. 'His clothes. Very new. Very expensive. He is in a big car from *Iraklion*. He take his mother away. She cry. She do not want to go, but he say come, I have money, you help me.'

'Where did they go?' asked Patrick, after a pause in which all the men looked away from him. They clearly feared that Yannis was engaged in a dubious enterprise and had involved his mother. 'Athens?'

No one answered. Then more excited talk broke out and what seemed to be further argument, though most Greek conversation was carried on at this pitch. Petros and one old man seemed to be urging one course against the rest, and in the end they prevailed. Petros spoke.

'The wife of Manouli—' a nod towards the oldest man — 'she is the friend of Ilena. She has a letter.' Pause. Patrick waited. 'She is on an island, doing work, but it is not hard. She has much comfort. Yannis is working for a shipping firm. He is well paid and can support her.'

'That's good, then.' But it was not, that was plain. The men did not approve of Yannis's new prosperity. Anyway, if he was thriving, there was no need to seek him out. 'Which island?' Patrick asked.

In the end they told him.

He drove away still puzzled by their reticence.

III

The ruins of the palace of Phaestos shimmered in the heat. All around the plateau on which it had been built the land fell away into the surrounding fertile plain; what a vantage point, and the peaceful citizens had built no fortifications three thousand years ago. Patrick wandered about in the hot sun among the thick, ancient walls trying to imagine the scene as it had been in those days, but not succeeding very well. Around him, clustering on the heels of their various guides, were flocks of tourists in bright dresses and shirts. Patrick heard French, German, Italian and English, and other tongues he could not recognize. He stood for a while gazing across at Mount Ida, allegedly Zeus's birthplace. And why not?

After a time he felt too hot to remain outside any longer, though he had not worked out the plan of the palace at all well in his mind. He had consumed a fair amount of ouzo with his new Cretan friends, for none of which had he been allowed to pay, and he had then driven on to the coast where he had found a *taverna* by the sea. There he had eaten fried fish and drunk iced beer. The effect of it all was soporific. He walked slowly back to the tourist building where he could have some sort of long, cool, non-alcoholic drink.

He was sitting in the shade eating an enormous apple and drinking lemonade when Ursula Norris appeared from within the building and saw him. She was chuckling away to herself.

'Hullo,' she said. 'So you got here. I am pleased to see you.' She was choking with suppressed mirth. 'Do you know, in this birthplace of civilization, where there was an elaborate plumbing system three thousand years ago, the ladies' loo today is still just a hole in the ground? What about that for the march of progress?'

'No — really?'

'Mm. One wouldn't give it a thought anywhere else in Europe — but here—' she grinned at him. 'I've a childish sense of humour,' she said.

'Let me get you a drink,' Patrick suggested.

'I'd love one, but there isn't time. We've got to go back to the coach,' said Ursula.

'Come back with me,' said Patrick. 'My car will be like an oven as I could find no tree to park it under, and the clutch is lousy, but you're very welcome.'

'Oh, that would be lovely. Could I?' Her pleasure was genuine. 'I'll tell our guardian.'

She moved away, and Patrick saw her speak to an earnest-looking young woman with dark, glossy hair, wearing an orange dress. Then she returned.

'That's fine. Those couriers have a terrible job. There's always someone who's difficult, or keeps the coach waiting. How lovely to desert them.'

Patrick saw George Loukas and his wife looking at postcards. George said something to Elsie and took her elbow. They began to walk slowly towards the coach park.

'Those two came with you?' he asked. 'I saw them waiting to be collected.'

'Who? Oh, the American couple. Yes. Do you know them?'

'I met him in Challika last night,' said Patrick. 'He's of Greek descent. This is a sentimental pilgrimage for him.'

'Oh, that's wonderful,' said Ursula.

'He was talking away in Greek,' Patrick said. 'I was quite surprised that a second-generation American citizen had kept it up.'

'It happens all the time,' said Ursula. 'They come back to retire, after working all their lives in the States, sometimes.'

They sat and talked about it while she drank lemonade and shared the remains of Patrick's apple, and waited till the coach had gone.

IV

Their way back went through Gortys, and although two coaches were parked in the shade at the side of the road there was no seething mob swarming among the ruins, so they stopped.

'Modern stuff, this,' said Patrick, surveying the theatre. 'Even I can tell a Roman brick when I see one. What a nice place.'

The site, set among its olive trees, was a peaceful spot that afternoon.

'They'll excavate it thoroughly, one day, no doubt,' said Ursula Norris as they walked towards the odeum, built of soft, rose-coloured brick, wherein the code of laws could be seen inscribed on the inner wall. 'They were an enlightened lot, in those days.'

'Yes.' Patrick had read it up the night before in his *Hellenic Traveller*.

The ruined church of St. Titus drew them, and when they reached it, there was George Loukas wandering around saying, 'My, would you believe it?' to the lambent air. He hailed Patrick.

'Hi, there. Isn't this just great?' he cried. 'My, we've had a wonderful day, haven't we, Elsie?'

Elsie was looking rather hot. She had a silk scarf tied around her head; her face was flushed; strong, freckled arms lightly covered with fine gold hairs emerged from her lime-green dress.

'We've seen a heck of a lot of ruins,' she said.

'Say, honey, what am I thinking of? You haven't met Dr Grant, have you?' George said. 'He's the professor from Oxford, England, I was telling you about. Let me present Mrs Loukas, Dr Grant.'

Patrick felt unequal to explaining at this point that he was not a professor. He shook hands with Elsie and introduced Ursula Norris to both the Americans.

'Did you read about the feller that found this place?' George continued enthusiastically. 'He was drinking from a stream when he saw a stone in the water that had been carved some special way. So he covered it up and said nothing till he was able to buy the ground years later. What a guy.'

'Archaeology is a patient profession,' said Ursula.

'It must be great when you make a find, eh?' said George. 'Good results are worth waiting for.'

'Have you visited Knossos yet, Mrs Loukas?' asked Patrick.

'No. I guess it's a whole lot better than Phaestos, though. Not so ruined,' said Elsie Loukas. She sounded completely American; many years in the States might well erase the strongest British accent.

'I can understand Sir Arthur Evans not wanting to go anywhere else, can't you?' said Ursula. 'I'd be quite happy to set up camp here, for instance, and start digging.'

'I guess it can be wet and cold in winter, Miss Norris, even in Crete,' said George.

The Loukases had to leave them, as their guide was calling her flock together.

'What a nice little man,' said Ursula, watching them go. 'She's had her fill of ruins, I think, don't you?'

Patrick agreed. They walked slowly back through the shaded grove to their car, which did not want to start. Patrick

53

grumbled about it as they bumped over the grass where they had left it, back to the road.

'Poor car. It's doing its best,' said Ursula. 'I expect it's had a different driver every week, all summer. I'm delighted to be in it, I can tell you. The coaches are comfortable, and it's an easy way to get about — but what a long day. They haven't finished yet — they'll be stopping somewhere else on the way back — Mallia, probably.'

'These trips just whet one's appetite, don't they?' said Patrick. 'Make one long to return.'

'Yes. It's all too quick. I'd like a whole day in the museum in Heraklion. I think the tour allows just over an hour. Even a day isn't enough, from what I've heard.'

'The famous Linear B tablet,' said Patrick. 'What a story that is.'

They discussed the solving of mysteries from the past as they drove on, the road climbing soon, back up to the mountains. Ursula Norris felt that she was lucky to have met this cultured, not-so-very-young man, who was lonely enough to be glad of her company.

'Crete — the modern bit — the war, and all that — keeps coming into my mind as much as the distant past,' said Patrick. 'An island of drama — ancient and modern.'

'It's typical of Greek history in general,' said Ursula. 'Perhaps it's what's given them their resilient character.'

They passed a vine-growing area where grapes were spread out on racks in the sun to dry into raisins, and through arid stretches where even goats must find cropping a livelihood hard. Occasionally they came upon a donkey carrying a black-clad woman, with often a goat or a sheep at its heels.

Back in Challika, Patrick suggested a drink, and said he wanted to buy a paper, so they parked the car and walked along to the newsagent's where Patrick bought *The Times* and Ursula *The Guardian*. Then they went to Zito's, where Ursula taught Patrick to order their ouzos with a whole sentence in Greek.

There was a small paragraph in *The Times* about Felix; it said merely that his body had been found on a beach in Crete and that he had died as the result of an accidental fall from the cliff while on holiday. There was no mention of the cruise. A few words followed about his academic achievements. Among the ordinary obituaries, Gwenda announced his death and the time of his funeral, four days hence.

'Poor old Felix.' Patrick shook his head. 'Gwenda hasn't wasted much space on him.'

Ursula thought eulogies, however well merited, over-doing things, and said so.

'She must have had an awful shock,' she pointed out.

'I don't suppose it's interrupted her life much,' said Patrick. 'She'll carry on just as before, but she'll wear a martyr's expression for a while.'

'You don't like her, do you?'

'No,' said Patrick flatly. Then he went on, changing the subject, 'I had an interesting time this morning trying to track down the Greek godson of another friend of mine who's just died.' He described his morning.

'Obviously Yannis has done something they don't approve of in Ai Saranda,' said Ursula.

'Yes. But what? I thought he'd got himself into some sort of political scrape — that's what Alec thought, I'm sure.'

'The old men might have been prudently evasive about that, if it were so, but they wouldn't have been disapproving,' said Ursula.

'That's what I thought. It was almost as if they were embarrassed,' said Patrick.

'When are you going to that island to look for him?'

'How did you know I'd do that?' Patrick looked at her in astonishment.

'Well, you'll soon be bored here, when you've been to Knossos and a few other spots. I'm sure you aren't content to lie in the sun for more than a day or two. Besides, I don't think you like loose ends, do you?'

'Am I so transparent?'

'No, but you're a positive sort of person. More impulsive, too, than many academics.'

'What about you?' Patrick attacked back, shaken by such discernment.

'Oh — I'm quite ordinary. I kept house for my father until he died last May. Now I'm having an indefinite holiday. I don't know when I'll go back to my job.'

'Where is that?'

'At the National Gallery.'

Patrick was about to ask her in what capacity, when his attention was distracted by a large black car which drove past and stopped outside the police station. Out got Inspector Manolakis, wiry and smart in his uniform. He spoke to the driver and disappeared within.

'Is that the local police chief?' Ursula asked.

'I don't know if he's the chief. He's the chap who's been dealing with poor old Felix. It must be very trying for the local force when tourists die.'

'Nice for the tourist, if he's happy,' Ursula said.

'Yes — if it happens peacefully, while you're sitting on the terrace looking at the sea. But not if you drown.' He would never forget Felix's appearance, ravaged by the effect of the water.

'Hullo — your policeman has seen you. He's coming to talk to you,' said Ursula.

Sure enough, Inspector Manolakis had emerged from the police station and was walking towards them.

'Good evening, Mr Grant. How are you?' he said. Patrick introduced Ursula, and the policeman repeated, 'How are you?' Greeks often used this greeting, Patrick had noticed.

'Won't you join us, Inspector?' he suggested. 'Can I get you a drink?'

'Thank you. I will have coffee, please,' said Manolakis.

The waiter, seeing him, had at once appeared, and now took the order with a sincere '*amesos*', returning in a magically short time with the strong Greek coffee for the policeman.

'Your friend, Mr Lomax — the matter is at rest,' he said. 'The body goes back to England tomorrow.'

'Oh, good.' Someone had been efficient. The unfortunate vice-consul, no doubt, summoned from Heraklion. 'It's reported briefly in the paper,' Patrick said, indicating his copy of *The Times*.

'So sad. You must forget it now and enjoy your holiday,' said Manolakis. He was looking at Patrick consideringly. 'You are in *Kriti* for fourteen days?'

'No. I'm going to Athens soon. Friday, probably.'

'Ah — you have been to Athens before?'

'Yes.'

They talked about Athens for a while, with Ursula and Patrick waxing lyrical and Manolakis proudly listening to their praises of the city, drinking his coffee.

'I am glad you like,' he said.

He left them then, and when he had gone the waiter rushed over to see if they had more commands.

'You're a marked man now,' said Ursula. 'The policeman's friend.'

'It was nice of him to talk to us,' said Patrick. 'I wonder why he did?'

'Just natural Greek courtesy.'

'I thought he was pleased that I was leaving,' Patrick said slowly. 'Now why? The business about Felix seems to be closed. They've decided it was an accident.'

'But you're not sure?'

'I think Manolakis is convinced it was suicide.'

'If it was—' Ursula hesitated, choosing her words. 'If it was, it's a terrible thing to have happened, and surely better by far for everyone's sake to have it officially described as accidental. You said your friend had a tiresome wife.'

Patrick laughed shortly.

'If every man with a tiresome wife killed himself the suicide rate would soar,' he said. 'I just don't see Felix doing such a thing. Besides, a man suffering from vertigo would choose another way of doing it, wouldn't he? He wouldn't throw himself over a cliff. And why here, anyway?'

V

'He'd had a lot to drink,' said Patrick.

They were sitting on the hotel terrace after dinner. Taped bouzouki music came from the softly-lit *taverna* bar outside which the tables were arranged. The scent from the flowers in the well-watered beds filled the air, and when briefly the bouzoukis stopped, the cicadas could be heard instead.

'He might not have realized he was close to the cliff edge, in the darkness,' said Ursula. 'He might just have blundered over it.'

'I've never seen a night in a place like this that was so dark,' said Patrick. Both remembered that when they had arrived the harbour lights were brilliantly reflected in the sea; and now the sky above them was full of stars. 'There's a moon at the moment — it's coming up to the full. And anyway, what was he doing here when he should have been sailing up to the Black Sea? That's what I'd like to know.' For by now he had told Ursula about Felix's cruise commitment.

'Had he no papers on him? Nothing that explained it?'

'No. Only a wallet with some money, and his driving licence. And his passport.'

'Have you got your passport on you now?' asked Ursula.

'No. It's locked in my case in my room. I don't carry it around all the time.'

'Neither do I. That's what I meant.'

'That he was in transit, so to speak? The police found no record of his having booked in anywhere, nor any luggage. I suppose he could have dumped it somewhere.'

'Are you going to tell Inspector Manolakis about his fear of heights?'

'I don't think so. Or not at the moment.'

'His wife must be satisfied with whatever explanation she's been given, or she'd make a fuss and demand further enquiries.'

'Mm. She may have had a letter from him, saying why he'd changed his plans.'

'Do you think, if it really were suicide, that he might have decided to do it in the most challenging way he could find?' By an act that terrified him in itself?' asked Ursula.

Patrick considered this.

'Interesting theory. It's possible, I suppose. But why come to Crete for it? I still find it impossible to accept Felix as a suicide.' He sighed. 'Still, what do we really know about anyone? It's all only guesswork. Maybe I just don't want to accept that a friend of mine could be in a state of despair and I hadn't noticed. Why don't we stop thinking about it for now, and go down to the town? Have you been there in the evening? It's quite lively.'

'I haven't, and I'd love to come,' said Ursula. 'I'll just get a sweater, if you don't mind waiting for a minute.'

She hastened off to her room, and while she was gone Patrick stood in the hotel foyer studying the notices which advertised trips to Knossos, Heraklion and so forth, and excursions by boat to various islands. It was pleasant to have found such a congenial companion; the little town was best enjoyed in company. How satisfactory to feel that there could be no emotional complications from their friendship.

Ursula soon returned. With her height and her striking white hair, she was a handsome woman.

He told her about *Aphrodite's*, the shop where he had bought Jane's waistcoat, and suggested she might like to go there before they had their drinks. Ursula agreed, and they parked the car near the foot of the steep steps leading to that part of the town. A few people were wandering about up there, but most of the activity was centred around the waterfront.

In the shop they found the mother still knitting, but the girl was attending to an elderly couple who were choosing a rug. Ursula at once began to browse among the crochet-work, telling Patrick he was quite right to enthuse about it.

'Will you be dreadfully bored, waiting?' she asked.

'Not a bit. We've all night before us,' said Patrick. 'Take your time.'

He started to look at postcards, and watched her covertly. She had a confident manner that was quite without arrogance; she clearly knew her own value and a lot about life. She hasn't just moved between her father's house and the Gallery, thought Patrick, and wondered about her elastic plan to stay in Greece indefinitely.

Little Sophia was struggling hard with the couple she was serving. They were carrying out their transaction in English but there was some difficulty about it, and it soon became obvious that they were German. The woman seemed to speak only a few words of English, but the man spoke more; his accent, though, was thick. Sophia's mother kept her eye on them, her needles for ever clicking but her glance was sharp.

While they were negotiating, George and Elsie Loukas came into the shop. George was delighted to see Patrick.

'Elsie would come here. Said it's cheaper than some of those shops down by the harbour,' he said. 'She wants one of those embroidered dresses. Look honey,' he addressed his wife, 'there's a whole rail of them here.'

Elsie began to look through a rack of long caftan-type dresses, and George, who had seen Sophia's mother at the back of the shop, started a conversation with her. She looked surprised at first, and then delighted. Still keeping an eye on her daughter, she actually laid down her knitting and joined in a busy dialogue.

The German woman had now decided she must add an embroidered caftan to her pile of purchases. She crossed to the rail where Elsie was looking through them. Neither took the least notice of the other but grimly pursued their quest. Elsie snatched out a black dress and held it against her body; the German woman looked annoyed and rattled the hangers as she hunted on. Sophia came anxiously across.

'You like what colour?' she asked the German woman.

'I want a black dress and this woman's taken the only one there is,' said the woman to her husband, speaking in German.

'I'll try this on,' Elsie said to Sophia. 'I found it first. If it doesn't fit, she can have it.'

'Of course. But I have more,' said Sophia. She bundled Elsie behind a curtain at the back of the shop with her booty, and then returned to the German woman. 'You would like a black one, please?' she said, and went to a shelf where more dresses, neatly folded, were stacked.

'Do you make these too?' Patrick asked.

'No. My sister makes them,' Sophia said.

'They're lovely. If I hadn't already got one, I'd buy one,' said Ursula. She turned and spoke to Sophia in Greek, and then added to Patrick, 'I said we'd come back when they're not so busy. She's got her hands full at the moment.'

It was true. Elsie had emerged from the curtained corner in her dress; her broad shoulders and impressive chest displayed the elaborate gold embroidery to perfection. The German woman now went behind the curtain to put hers on, while George told Elsie she looked magnificent.

'Doesn't she?' he appealed to Ursula and Patrick.

They agreed that she did.

'Like Brunhilde,' said Ursula.

The two walked back down the steep steps to the harbour and wandered on past the tables of the various *tavernas* and the *kafenia*. Patrick looked at the boats tied up below the wall.

'There's an interesting set-up,' he said, and pointed out the *Psyche* at her berth. 'A sweet young Canadian girl seems to be helping a Greek lad with that boat on its trips.'

'What fun for her,' said Ursula mildly.

'I thought it would be pleasant to have a day with them exploring the coast. But I'm not sure if there will be time now.'

'You're going after Yannis?'

'Yes. That, and other things.' Patrick stared at the *Psyche*. 'Come on, let's find a table.'

Though it was still warm, the air was fresh now, and everyone seemed to have woken up. From Zito's came the sound of bouzoukis.

'It's curiously haunting music, isn't it?' said Ursula. 'Lilting and gay, yet with a melancholy undertone.'

'Like the Greek character.'

'Yes.'

'I suppose all this tourism is a good thing. Brings prosperity.'

'Oh, undoubtedly. But the young people find it pays better to work in the hotels rather than on the land. That seems a pity.'

A couple whom Patrick recognized as being a youthful pair from the hotel went past.

'The place is packed with honeymooners,' he said tartly.

'Don't you think it's an ideal spot for romance?' Ursula suggested.

'I suppose so,' said Patrick in a surly tone.

'Sunlight and tranquillity. What more can you want when you're young and in love?' said Ursula, watching the pair walk slowly along, hand in hand. 'Penzance in the rain wouldn't be quite the same.'

'I suppose not. Look, there's the Canadian girl I told you about,' said Patrick, seizing the chance to change the subject.

Jill McLeod had emerged from Zito's and was walking along the quay towards the boat. She wore a long skirt in some purple flowered material, and a tight black top. Her hair, freed from its pony-tail, was loose and flowing.

'Is that the boat owner with her?'

A young man was following Jill. He was small and dark, but he was older than Spiro and had a moustache.

'No.'

He could have been the man who was with Jill and Spiro the night Patrick first saw them, but he was not sure. They both went down the steps and aboard the *Psyche*, and disappeared into the cabin.

'I wonder if she's living on board that boat with those two young men,' Ursula said. She sounded interested.

'Probably, said Patrick. He was not sure that the second young man was a permanent part of the crew.

'Well, she's got it the right way round — two men and a girl,' said Ursula.

A few minutes later Spiro appeared on the quayside and hurried aboard after the other two. Ten minutes afterwards the boat cast off her moorings and chugged out of the harbour towards the open sea.

VI

The next day Patrick and Ursula went to Knossos, calling at the museum in Heraklion on the way. They started early ahead of the coach, and had one of the few perfect days of a lifetime, reaching the museum before the main crowds so that they had time to enjoy the vivid frescoes. They stayed there till it closed at one o'clock and both said they would return if they had the chance another time.

'Lunch now. I'm very hungry,' said Ursula, and taught Patrick how to say it in Greek.

They sought about for a good spot and eventually found a *taverna* in a street leading down to the harbour. There was a shady garden with tables arranged under a vine.

They chose *tarasamalata* followed by *dolmades*.

'A very Greek meal, so it should be good. Sometimes Greek food is disappointing,' Ursula remarked.

'I've discovered that,' said Patrick.

'Never mind. Love the Greeks and love their food, even when it's tough and tepid,' said Ursula. 'I am enjoying myself.'

They finished their meal with fruit and coffee, then, before going back to the car, they walked along the road past the harbour. Two cruise liners were in, their upper-works gleaming white against the skyline. The shops were closed now and would not re-open until four o'clock, or even later. The whole town rested in the heat. Patrick saw a female figure in a pair of brief, frayed cotton shorts walking along the road in front of them.

'There's Jill. The Canadian girl from the *Psyche*,' he said.

'Is it? Are you sure?'

Patrick would have recognized her shape anywhere.

'Yes. I'm sure.'

The girl took a turning to the right and walked off towards the centre of the town. She had a long, loping stride that was very graceful.

'The boat wasn't in the harbour when we left this morning. We saw them put out last night, if you remember.'

'Do you think they came here all the way by sea?' asked Ursula.

'Why not? I suppose it's the obvious way, when you think about it,' Patrick said.

PART THREE:
FRIDAY AND SATURDAY

ATHENS AND THE ISLAND

I

Patrick flew to Athens in the morning. Before he left Crete, Ursula Norris gave him the telephone number of a villa near Vouliagmeni where she would be the following week, and he promised to ring her.

'We'll probably meet by chance in the museum or somewhere, anyway,' she said. 'I hope we do.'

'So do I,' said Patrick, and meant it.

Their afternoon at Knossos had been an enchantment to them both. Aided by Sir Arthur Evans's reconstructions and the paintings they had seen in the museum, they were able to imagine the palace as it was. They had wandered about the site for over two hours and pitied the visitors from the cruise liners who spent only fifteen minutes there. In the evening they dined in Challika, and this time there was mullet.

The *Psyche* was not yet back at her mooring.

'I suppose it would take her some time,' said Ursula.

'An hour. More, perhaps. I don't know how many knots she'd do,' said Patrick. 'As long as the sea was calm it should be an easy trip — no winding about like the road.'

'There's the little girl from the shop — Sophia, did you say her name was? We've never been back there,' said Ursula.

She was looking across the road, and Patrick followed her gaze. Sophia had come down the steps between the buildings. She crossed the road and stood on the quayside looking at the boats. Then she stared out to sea. Finally she walked right round the harbour to the very end of the jetty, from where she could look beyond the confines of the bay to the open sea. She stayed there for some time, and then walked back slowly, dejection in every line of her body.

'Mama must be in charge of the shop tonight,' said Patrick. 'I wonder if Sophia's looking for the *Psyche?*'

'Maybe. But I expect there are other boats, and other young men besides Spiro and his friend,' said Ursula.

The next morning, as he drove past on his way to the airport where he had arranged to surrender the car, Patrick paused at the harbour and looked towards the *Psyche's* mooring-place. She was still away.

Athens was hot, dusty, and very noisy.

In the plane Patrick had felt a mild nostalgia for Crete and his utilitarian room at the Hermes; he had grown used to the town of Challika, and the whole tempo of the place. But he was no closer to finding Yannis, and more days spent idling would diminish his resolution. However, all feelings of regret fled when he saw the Parthenon again. It must, he thought, be the most beautiful building in the world. He had booked a room at a hotel just off Constitution Square, which was central and convenient. From it he could discover how to get to the island of Mikronisos, and he could go to Delphi to intercept the *Persephone* when she called at Itea on Monday. It was this, much more than the search for Yannis, which was driving him now. He must try to discover why Felix left the ship; someone from among her crew or passengers might know.

He checked in at the hotel and was shown to a small cell with a tiny balcony overlooking a well between the inner walls of the building. More balconies were ranged in tiers all round. The city was full of tourists; he was lucky to find a room in such a central hotel at such short notice, and one that was away from the street, where the noise was unabating all round the clock.

Half an hour after his arrival he was sitting under a mulberry tree in the Plaka, at a *taverna* just below the great bulk of the Acropolis, with an iced beer and a salad lunch.

This was more like it.

Though it was the hottest part of the day now when life, in theory, came to a halt, there were still people about. A flow of tourists eddied up and down the wide flight of steps past the *taverna*. The buildings baked in the heat but it was cool under the big, spreading tree. Patrick felt his whole system shifting into faster gear after the torpor of the last few days in Crete.

There would be a ferry boat from the Piraeus to Mikronisos, he supposed. He wondered how best to pursue his enquiries when he got there. The unforthcoming attitude of the old men in Ai Saranda made him favour a furtive approach; it might not be prudent to ask for Yannis Pavlou outright. Anyway, there would be time to go there before he need be in Delphi to meet the *Persephone*. He would spend at least one night on Parnassus. The people from the ship would have a mere five hours up there, and Patrick knew from an earlier visit that this was not enough; but no doubt it was convenient to take your hotel with you wherever you went, with experts like Felix to bring the famous places to life in their lectures. He wished he knew more about ancient stones himself.

He finished his meal, and, profiting from Ursula's tuition, asked for the bill in Greek. Then he went down Diaskouron and through the streets of the old town towards Ermou. The heat was scorching, but he strode out briskly, his head protected by his Cretan straw hat. Every now and then he turned around to look for the Acropolis; the bulk of it loomed perpetually above the city, drawing the eye to the white temple there that was sometimes tinged with gold. He turned right and lost it behind the tall buildings of the modern city. Cars sped past with horns tooting and tyres squealing. In spite of the heat there were still crowds in the centre; tourist buses went by, and yellow trolley buses, and he saw the blue local buses too. The city seemed well served by public transport. He knew that every incoming bus converged upon Constitution Square but he had made no forays by bus in an outward direction from there when he was in Athens before.

That reminded him.

He had promised to put flowers on Miss Amelia Brinton's grave in the main cemetery when next he came to Athens. Her life-long friend, to whom he had made the promise, was now dead too. It seemed to Patrick that he had become hung about with obligations to the dead, the others much less easy to discharge than this one, which was merely a question of time and drachmas.

He hailed a taxi. It was too hot to walk to the cemetery.

The driver, a huge man with enormous shoulders like the bull of Minos himself, was amiable, and understood Patrick's diffident '*Nekrotafaeion, parakalo*,' without any trouble. His cab was adorned with artificial flowers, charms, and religious emblems, and he drove with such verve that Patrick felt it was prudent of him to have thrown out a few spiritual anchors.

There were flower stalls, Patrick knew, at the entrance to the cemetery. Beside the huge gates he saw gladioli, Michaelmas daisies and dahlias like those Miss Brinton had grown in her cottage garden. He bought an armful of white gladioli and blue daisies; they would die at once in the heat, but he would have fulfilled his promise.

Carrying them, he walked through the wide gateway into the cemetery and along the main path. He had forgotten what an immense place this was, but in spots it was shady for it was thickly planted with trees. Right down the middle, he seemed to remember, past a central building that looked like a chapel, and then somewhere up a pathway to the left lay the protestant section. There was a choice of turnings, and he made several errors before he found the right one. Eventually he came to Miss Brinton's last resting-place. A simple cross bearing her name and the dates of her birth and her death now marked the spot.

He laid the flowers on the grave and stood there for a moment. It was well-tended; the whole place was curiously peaceful and not at all sad. He moved away at last, and saw nearby an open grave, freshly dug, the dry stony soil in a heap at the side of it. As Patrick turned to go a very thin young man in a linen jacket and wearing a clerical collar appeared among the headstones and walked towards the empty grave, looking anxious. Patrick absently glanced at him, then looked more closely, and at the same time the young man saw him.

'Good Lord! Dr Grant,' he exclaimed.

'That sounds like an invocation, Jeremy,' said Patrick. 'What are you doing here? You look troubled.'

'I am. I'm walking the course, as it were,' said Jeremy Vaughan. 'I've got to take a funeral service her tomorrow.'

Patrick stared at the hole in the ground.

'Yes, that's right,' said Jeremy.

He had started his undergraduate life as a pupil of Patrick's, later switching subjects when he decided to go into the church. Patrick had lost track of his subsequent movements.

'Are you working in Athens? Attached to the Embassy?'

'No. I'm here with a group actually, doing the sites, you know. A W.E.A. party. The regular chaplain's away just now, so when this happened to one of our party it seemed obvious that I should step in. It's a bit different from Croydon.'

'I'm sure it is.' Patrick looked round at the pines and the dry, dusty ground. 'I came to a funeral here once,' he said. 'That's why I'm here today.'

'Oh, I see.' Jeremy looked across at the flowers on the other grave. 'A sad affair, I suppose.'

'Yes. But a nice funeral, if they ever are.'

'There's this lengthy procession,' said Jeremy doubtfully. 'All the way from the gate. It's miles.'

'I think someone leads the way,' said Patrick helpfully. 'You shouldn't get lost. The undertakers must be used to it. It was all quite casual and friendly, that part of it, I remember. Whose funeral is it?'

'A man called Dermott Murcott. He fell while climbing up a hill on Mikronisos.'

'Mikronisos?' Patrick looked up sharply. 'The island?'

'Yes. Do you know it?'

'I've heard of it.'

'It's a pretty spot — rather bare — not much vegetation. He was clambering about looking at lava formations in the rocks or something — it's full of volcanic traces — and he fell.'

'Did you see it happen?'

'No. No one did. He'd wandered away from the group. Everyone else was bathing. It took ages to find him.'

'How dreadful,' said Patrick.

'I heard about Dr Lomax. It was in the *Athens News*. That was terrible too,' said Jeremy. 'Rather the same sort of thing, in a way.'

'Yes, I suppose it was,' said Patrick.

They began to walk slowly back along the path. Jeremy was very small and slight, with steel-framed spectacles through which a pair of blue eyes gazed out at the world with assumed severity. He looked youthful in the extreme. Patrick remembered him coxing the Mark's Third Eight in a determined attempt to progress higher up the river. He had been, in those days, an admirable but much too serious young man, and seemed unaltered.

'I thought of going to Mikronisos tomorrow. Is it easy to get there?' Patrick asked.

'Oh yes. You get a steamer from Piraeus. It calls at some other islands first. Takes just over two hours.'

'Every day?'

'I think so — in the season anyway. But don't take my word for it. Better check it.'

'Tell me about the island. What's special about it?'

'Nothing, really.'

'Why did you go there?'

'Well, it's easy to reach, and it makes a change from the ordinary tourist run to Aegina and Hydra — we'd already done that. It's been so hot that we ditched some of our pre-arranged excursions and added a few that weren't so tiring. People were wilting all over the place. They're quite elderly, most of them,' said Jeremy.

'Are you in charge?'

'No. There's a retired headmaster leading the party, called Gareth Hodgson. I'm helping. It makes a holiday for me,' said the young man.

'Where are you staying?'

'At the Livingstone. It's near Omonia Square.'

'Oh yes. The Leicester Square of Athens,' said Patrick.

'I suppose it is. It's less salubrious than the Constitution Square area, certainly,' said Jeremy. 'But it's good value. The hotel's comfortable and the food's good. The trouble is it's such a trek to get anywhere. Some of the old dears are exhausted before we begin. Handy for the Archaeological Museum, though. You've been there, of course.'

'Indeed I have, and I'll be going again,' said Patrick.

'First thing in the morning's the best time. Before the hordes descend,' said Jeremy in avuncular tones.

'I'll remember.'

They turned into the main path and walked on towards the gate. A gardener went past carrying a rake, and ahead a priest of the Orthodox Church, cassock billowing, strode along, his little bun of grey hair neat under the rim of his stovepipe hat.

'They always look such fine fellows, Greek priests,' said Jeremy wistfully. 'All tall, with magnificent beards.'

Patrick, over six feet tall himself, could think of no cheering reply to this. It was perfectly true, he could not remember seeing a small *papa*.

'Tell me more about Mikronisos,' he urged. 'Is it inhabited?'

'Yes, but not on any great scale. There's a *taverna* by the jetty, and a few tourist shops, and a small church and some fishermen's cottages. And a few villas on the west coast. We didn't see them. You reach them by boat. There's no road. The church is interesting. Bits of it are Byzantine. There are traces of mosaic on one wall. It was a thriving place once, some sort of trading post, but there aren't any notable ruins.'

'Maybe they need to be found,' said Patrick. 'I expect there are fragments under most of these places.'

'Probably,' agreed Jeremy.

'How about dining with me tonight, Jeremy?' Patrick suggested. He could pump him further about the island over a meal. Without realizing it, Jeremy might have seen Yannis or Ilena or noticed some interesting feature of life on the island that could be significant.

'Oh, that would have been nice, but I can't desert the group,' said Jeremy. 'Their morale is a bit low, as you'll understand, after the accident,' he added gloomily. Then he brightened. 'Couldn't you dine with us instead? It would cheer them all up to meet someone new,' he said.

'I'll accept with pleasure,' said Patrick. He had no other plans.

'The moon's full tonight. The Acropolis is open then. Have you seen it by moonlight?' Jeremy asked.

'No. Oh, that's something that must be done. You tuck up your old dears after dinner and we'll go.'

'A few of them want to come,' sighed Jeremy. 'They can't possibly walk. We'll have to get taxis.'

'They don't cost much,' said Patrick. 'It's not like London.'

'True. We use the buses most of the time but they get crowded, and you have to move along during the journey, you know, from the back where you get in to the front where you get off. It's a bit tough if you're over seventy and not nimble.'

'That's why you see so many little old Greek ladies nipping into taxis in Athens,' said Patrick.

Jeremy's company was making him feel as elderly as the people he described; he realized that he had been subconsciously cast back by Jeremy into the role of tutor and sustainer. Poor Jeremy: worn down by all his responsibilities, he needed a crutch, and any spiritual one he claimed was not enough just now. He looked at the perspiring figure beside him. Jeremy would walk, in this heat, all the way back to his hotel, or anyway to Constitution Square where, with his local expertise, he doubtless knew the right bus-stop.

'I'm having a taxi to Constitution Square. Can I give you a lift? You can catch a bus from there to Omonia, can't you?' he said.

'Oh yes. On Venizelou. You have to remember how the one-way streets work. Then it's easy,' said Jeremy.

The fellow was an animated guide-book. Patrick paid off the taxi outside the King George Hotel, where he sank into a chair and commanded a long, cooling drink while Jeremy scuttled away round the corner in search of his bus.

'Two and a half drachs takes you anywhere,' he cried as he went.

Patrick remembered being told by Jeremy years before where to get shoes repaired at the lowest price in Oxford, and of other simple economies. He had been born thrifty, which was fortunate, for he was too earnest and humble ever to win earthly riches.

The hotel porter knew all about the boats to Mikronosis; one sailed at nine-thirty every morning and returned in the evening. Patrick would go the following day. He asked the man, who spoke very good English, to find him a hotel room in Delphi for Sunday night. He would hire a car and drive up there to wait in the mountains for the *Persephone*.

With all this arranged, he went up to his room to shower and shave.

It was almost worth getting tired and over-heated for the sheer sensuous pleasure of reviving under a stream of cool water. Much refreshed, Patrick went out on to his balcony. Lights were on in several rooms, although he had not yet switched on his own. Through some windows, where the net curtains were open, a clear view of the interior was revealed.

Patrick saw four intertwined legs on a bed in one room. He looked away, and across the well from him, on the same level, he saw a thick-set middle-aged man with curly grey hair standing in the room opposite, with a drink in his hand. He turned and moved from Patrick's sight; it appeared as if he were talking as he went. In a moment he came back into view, and there was another man with him, wearing a blue shirt. They talked together and the second man was given a drink, which he swallowed quickly. Then the first man took something from a drawer and gave it to the other, who put it in a small holdall. They talked together for a few minutes, then shook hands, and the second man left.

Patrick went downstairs too.

II

Patrick sat at a table in the middle of Constitution Square and ordered a beer. It was too early to go to Jeremy's hotel, and it was pleasant to sit watching the people passing. Men selling lottery tickets moved between the tables, and there was a sponge-seller with a string of pale sponges slung over his shoulder like a balloonman. Rather reluctantly Patrick rose at last to keep his appointment.

He turned down Venizelou as Jeremy had instructed and caught a bus a little way down the street. He got off where the roads converged on Omonia Square with its central fountains and subway entrances to the metro. There were more lottery tickets for sale here; the smell of cooking and petrol vapours filled the air, and the night was full of noise. The surging crowds were well-drilled, waiting for the pedestrian lights to change to green before crossing the streets, and ruled also by smart policemen with shrill whistles. Numerous roads radiated from the hub of the square, and Patrick consulted his map to make sure he was choosing the right one. It was easy to lose one's bearings at this point. All the streets were well marked, however, and he walked on round the square till he came to Konstantinou. It was a wide street, sloping gently downwards; the hotel was almost at the end of it.

Jeremy was waiting for him in the foyer.

'We're all in the bar upstairs. I saw you from the window,' he said. He had shed his clerical collar and was wearing a narrow black tie, a plain white shirt and a blazer. He looked about eighteen, but cooler now and less worried. 'I had a swim when I got back,' he said. 'Very refreshing.'

'Is there a pool here?'

'Yes — on the roof. It gets very hot up there — all the concrete, you know, and the air-conditioning. Hot waves come out of pipes all round you. They say Athens is getting hotter and hotter because of the petrol fumes and the air-conditioning.'

It sounded likely. Jeremy was a fund of informative theory.

'It's terribly noisy,' he added. 'They're tearing down some building or other at the back, and the bulldozers start work at about six in the morning.'

'They're always tearing down bits of Athens and putting them back again,' said Patrick, and then hoped he hadn't sounded patronizing. After all, he'd only been here once before himself.

Thirty-three people, most of them elderly and female, sat on black mock-leather chairs in a corner of the bar. There were two young women among them, one thin with long, lank brown hair, the other plump, with glasses and severe acne. Patrick shook hands with everyone as Jeremy introduced them. Gareth Hodgson, the leader, was a thin man with faded fair hair threaded with grey and gold-rimmed half-spectacles. He looked very frail.

One of the men in the group wore a blue shirt and had thinning grey hair; Patrick had seen him not an hour before across the well of his own hotel in the opposite room. He must have had to wait some minutes for the lift, for Patrick, who had gone down the stairs himself, had seen him emerge, carrying a BEA holdall, as he came into the foyer.

His name was Arthur Winterton. When they were introduced he gave no sign of having seen Patrick before.

III

One long table was reserved for the party in the restaurant. The meal was good, with roast chicken, beans, and the ubiquitous chips. Conversation was muted. Occasionally someone laughed, then looked abashed, as though an improper remark had been made. Patrick sat next to Gareth Hodgson, who took one end of the table; Jeremy went to the other end, and Patrick saw the thin young woman with the lank hair rush to sit next to him. The plump girl was following them when Mr Hodgson called her and invited her to sit on Patrick's right. This was clearly intended as a privilege, and the girl, whose name was Celia Watson, blushed and looked pleased; she obeyed, but throughout the meal Patrick noticed that she cast jealous glances towards the foot of the table. By the time the meal ended he was sure it was her female friend, not Jeremy, about whom she was most concerned.

She taught history at a comprehensive school; the grammar school where Gareth Hodgson had been headmaster had been welded into it. They talked about teaching through the first two courses of dinner. Celia was an awkward, gauche girl, but she was interested in her work. Patrick was eager to turn the conversation towards the incident on Mikronisos but there seemed to be an agreement among the party to avoid the subject. In the end, while Mr Hodgson was answering some point about the journey home on Sunday raised by the elderly woman sitting on his left, Patrick asked Celia if she had known the dead man well.

'Oh no. I'd never met him before this holiday,' she said. 'We don't all come from the same study group at home.'

'Was he married?' There had seemed to be no grieving widow among the ladies he had met before dinner.

'No. Or at least, maybe he was a widower.'

'A sad business.'

'Yes. It was dreadful. Until the accident, we'd been having one of our best days,' said Celia. 'It was such a good idea to hire a boat and go round to the quiet part of the island. Most visitors don't go further than the harbour.'

'I'm planning to go there tomorrow,' said Patrick. 'You recommend it, do you?'

'Oh, certainly.'

The waiter came between them then, and Patrick glanced at the row of people facing them across the long table. They were all at least a generation older than Celia. Among them sat Arthur Winterton, steadily eating; he seemed concerned only with his food and was making no effort to talk to the grey-haired ladies on either side of him.

Patrick asked about Celia's university career and dragged out of her the details of her good degree. He managed to keep her attention concentrated for a full five minutes before she looked towards the other girl and Jeremy again. Then she saw that Patrick had noticed her glance and blushed. The ugly pimples showed dark against her over-heated, sunburnt skin.

Later, with the two girls, Jeremy, and five of the others, he set out for the Acropolis. Arthur Winterton and Gareth Hodgson were among those who stayed behind saying they wanted an early night.

Outside the hotel they stood on the kerb while the traffic tore past with screeching tyres and blaring horns, hoping to secure two taxis. A free one came along at last and stopped at their signals. Jeremy shepherded three elderly ladies into the back seat; then there was a discussion about who should go with them. There was space for another passenger beside the driver.

'You come, Mr Vaughan,' pleaded one old lady. 'Please. We won't be able to manage the money without you.'

Jeremy grimaced. By the end of two weeks, surely they could sort out a few drachmas?

'All right—' he looked doubtfully at Patrick.

'We'll find you up there,' said Patrick cheerfully. 'We'll meet you at the entrance.'

'Right.'

Jeremy was about to get in beside the driver when the second girl, whose name Patrick could not remember, slid in under his arm and moved up behind the gear lever.

'There's room for me too,' she said, and added rudely but truthfully, 'We're thinner than any of you.'

Unless they were to have three taxis, five of them must travel together. But Patrick, already turned away watching for another cab, saw the expression on Celia's face as Jeremy clambered in next to the girl.

Celia saw that she had given herself away.

'She's so blatant,' she said, scowling. 'She runs after him all the time.'

They were both a little apart from their two older companions who were thankfully leaving to them the task of capturing transport.

'I don't think Jeremy's noticed at all, if it's any comfort to you,' Patrick said, and stepped out into the road, gesturing, as another taxi appeared.

There were only a few people making their way up the steps at the start of the climb up the Acropolis when they reached it. Jeremy and his group were waiting for them by the gate through which the public were admitted, and they all began the ascent together. Wooden steps had been built under the great Propylaea since Patrick's last visit; he felt a sense of violation as he walked on them; they might be safer, but they brought a utilitarian note to a scene that should not have one.

Pale in the moonlight, the columns of the Parthenon took on a new dimension; voices were hushed; figures looked spectral. It was easy to imagine the presence of Plato or of Sophocles.

Patrick found that the wretched Celia, sensing sympathy, something she must rarely attract, had attached herself to him.

'I shouldn't have said that, back at the hotel,' she mumbled.

'It's all right. No one else heard you,' he said. 'Mind you don't fall.' He took her elbow as she seemed about to stumble over a lump of marble right in front of her. 'Are you colleagues — you and — I'm afraid I didn't catch your friend's name?'

'Joyce Barlow. Yes. We met at college,' said Celia. 'We always go on holiday together.' She stared at the boulder-strewn ground. 'It happens every year.'

What could he say to comfort her? Her life would always be like this.

'Forget it now,' he said. 'Look around you. You'll come to Athens again, I'm sure, but perhaps not when the moon is full.'

The miserable, spotty girl took a crumpled handkerchief out of her handbag and blew her nose. Then she made an effort to appreciate the scene.

'It's very fine,' she said.

Patrick felt a sudden wish for the company of Ursula Norris, who had found irony at Phaestos. Now here was he, on the Acropolis of Athens in the moonlight, with a plain, fat, pimpled girl who seemed to have lesbian leanings. It was difficult to laugh at such things alone.

He managed gradually to manoeuvre Celia towards the others, intending to offload her if he could.

'Oh Joyce, there you are, where have you been?' cried Celia bossily when she saw the other girl. 'Come and look at the eastern pediment.'

She'd never learn, poor creature, Patrick thought. Friendship was not enough for her; she must possess. And she seemed bent on masochism. He turned his back on them all and wandered away towards the Belvedere, where he stood gazing out across the lights of the city at Lykabettos, rising like a jewel above its floodlit diadem; it looked entrancing. He had been to its summit in daylight, never at night. He stood in silence; the air, cool now, brushed his face; there was always a breeze up here. Was he imagining that he could smell the scent of thyme from the hills? Could there be another place in the world as mysteriously compelling as this city of the old and new? If so, he had never been there, nor wished to find one.

He turned reluctantly away; he must join the others. People moved about slowly; it was impossible to recognize anyone from a distance. An American voice rang out, close by, discussing allergies. 'My kid can't tolerate talcum,' he heard incongruously.

Patrick walked towards the great temple. Figures passed in and out among its columns and climbed up and down its steps. Two men wandered along together, talking. As Patrick passed them the moonlight revealed their faces. One, thickset and middle-aged, was the man he had seen earlier in his hotel with Arthur Winterton; the second was the young man with a moustache who had been with Jill and Spiro aboard the *Psyche*.

IV

Celia and Joyce were not talking at breakfast. Joyce had spoken her mind after Celia had received a telephone call from Patrick at eight o'clock.

'You should go to the funeral, Celia. We all ought to be there. It's a matter of respect.'

'I'd never met Dermott Murcott two weeks ago, and nor had you. He won't notice,' said Celia flatly.

She hoped Joyce was jealous. A man, and a proper one, twice the size of weedy Jeremy, had invited her out for the day. Patrick Grant wanted her to go with him to Mikronisos. No delusions about his reason for this filled Celia's mind; the motive was practical, she knew, and thought it was because he had formed a good opinion of her intellect.

'Everyone else will be there,' Joyce went drearily on.

'Then I won't be missed,' said Celia.

'It's not fair to Jeremy. He needs support.'

'Oh well, of course, if you're thinking of him and not Dermott Murcott—'

'It's all the same thing,' said Joyce.

On this note they went in to breakfast and had been sitting there in silence for ten minutes when Jeremy arrived. No one else had yet appeared.

'Oh Jeremy, come and sit down,' said Joyce, brightening visibly. She patted the seat beside her.

'I'm terribly late,' said Jeremy, who was usually the first at the table.

Patrick had returned to the hotel with him the previous night. They had said goodnight to the rest of his flock, and even Joyce and Celia had drifted off to bed, though not without a few wistful backward glances as the two men retreated into the bar. They had had several drinks together at Patrick's expense and Jeremy had overslept by half an hour as a result; an unprecedented event.

'What time do we leave?' asked Joyce. 'The funeral's at ten-thirty isn't it?'

'Yes. A quarter to ten will be plenty of time. You'll have to get taxis — it's too far to walk and there's no direct bus from here.' Jeremy's worries, which had temporarily receded, loomed again. 'Mr Hodgson will collect everyone together downstairs. I'm going on ahead.'

'Of course you must. I'll come with you, shall I?' offered Joyce.

'Oh, it's very kind of you, Joyce, but no, thank you,' said Jeremy, aghast at the very idea. He must have a chance to compose himself. 'You'd help much more by keeping an eye on Mrs Dawson. I'm anxious about her already, and if it gets hot she'll feel faint. Perhaps when the service in the chapel is over you could persuade some of them not to follow to the grave. It isn't necessary, and it's a long walk through the cemetery. There are seats about the place. They could wait in the shade.'

Joyce did not care for this girl-guide role, but she was willing to accept any crumb Jeremy might cast in her direction.

'Don't worry about a thing,' she said. 'I'll do my best. Celia's not coming, though. Your friend Dr Grant is taking her out for the day.'

'What?' Even Jeremy gaped at this disclosure.

'He's fetching her at a quarter to nine and they're off to Mikronisos on the boat,' said Joyce. 'I thought you'd be surprised. She should be coming to the funeral.'

'Oh, it doesn't matter about the funeral,' said Jeremy, rallying. 'There'll be quite enough people there as it is. I wish some of the others would stay away.' What could Patrick be thinking of? 'How nice for you, Celia,' he added lamely.

Patrick must have some deep reason. He had pumped him, Jeremy now recalled, about the whole group over their drinks the night before, asking what he knew about each of them and whose idea it had been to go to Mikronisos in the first place. Jeremy could not remember.

'There's no need for you to be at the funeral, Celia,' he assured her again. 'You were splendid after the accident.'

For she had been: it was she who had approached the body, pronounced it dead, fetched help, and comforted the shocked companions; and she had shown much good sense during the following troubled hours.

Celia perked up at this praise, and Joyce looked sulky.

'Well, at least we won't have to put up with your moods all day,' she muttered, too quietly for Jeremy to hear.

Celia did not reply. She got up and left the dining-room. Already her dress, strained across her heavy bosom, was stained with sweat under her armpits.

Patrick arrived five minutes early, but she was ready. He beamed upon her. He was making use of her, true, but he meant to give her an enjoyable day if he could. His heart sank slightly at her appearance, but he was accustomed to finding the sound kernels of unattractive nuts, and there was something to be said for a condition of utter safety from emotional or erotic risk. Their taxi took them swiftly to the Piraeus and past the liner dock to where the island ferries were berthed. Both had brought bathing things, and Patrick carried binoculars. There was quite a crowd pushing aboard their boat: old ladies in black; young men in short-sleeved, open-necked shirts; girls in bright dresses; a dog on a lead held by a middle-aged woman with a small boy; a crate of squawking chickens; men with bicycles. Patrick, guided by the hotel porter, had bought first-class tickets, and they went up to the top deck to watch the embarkation. The boat had moved from the quay and was thudding on towards open water when a voice hailed Patrick.

'Why, hullo there! So we meet again!'

George and Elsie Loukas, she with her head tied up in a green silk scarf and wearing dark glasses, were at the rail.

V

It was apparent that George and Elsie were delighted to meet Patrick again. They greeted Celia with warmth, and related what they had done since leaving Crete; they had eaten some good meals, been to Sounion, and looked up some distant cousins of George's.

'Elsie felt a little out of things, I guess, not speaking Greek,' George said. 'My cousins don't speak any English.'

The Loukases were visiting Mikronisos because Elsie's first husband had been there before the war and said it was an interesting place.

'She's still a bit edgy,' George confided to Patrick while the two women were discussing education in the States. 'I'd planned this part of our trip to be as meaningful for her as for me. I know she thinks about that first husband of hers even yet. I'm not jealous — why should I be? He's dead and I'm not. Maybe I thought if she saw the country where he died and some of the spots that had impressed him in his lifetime it would — oh, I don't know, kind of lay his ghost.' He looked a little sheepish as he said this, but he was not Greek for nothing; he saw no need to deny emotion. 'We've got no kids, you see,' he added. 'Elsie had one, with her first husband. It died. So it must be on account of me.'

Patrick thought that this was not necessarily true, but he felt unable to reply. However, George was continuing.

'We'd thought of going to Hydra — the tourist run, it is that trip — but we can go there some other time. If we get back to New Jersey without seeing this island she might regret it later. Say,' he lowered his voice, 'what are you doing with that girl?'

Were they really so incongruous a pair? Patrick decided not to tease George but to answer with the truth.

'She's had a row with her friend and needs to get away,' he said. 'And I want her to show me the island. She's been there before.' He told George about Dermott Murcott's accident.

'You're a morbid sort of guy, aren't you?' George said. 'Going to look at the scene of the crime.'

'It was an accident,' Patrick said.

George was looking at him shrewdly.

'It was?'

'Oh yes. No doubt of it. How could it be anything else?' said Patrick blandly. 'He slipped.'

They reached Mikronisos at last, having left most of their passengers at a larger island on the way. The few houses and shops on the waterfront shone in the brilliant sunlight as the ship nosed in to the jetty. All were freshly painted, most of them white, but some were pink or blue; the mellow tiled roofs glowed in contrast. There was a small *kafenion* and a *taverna* which advertised sea-food. The Loukases, Celia and Patrick were all thirsty, so before exploring they found a table in the shade and ordered drinks. George took charge of the proceedings.

'I wonder if the people who live here were all born on the island?' Patrick enquired with an innocent air as the waiter wiped their table down.

George at once asked the waiter, who replied volubly. He was young, with an alert expression and smiling brown eyes. How odd of Celia to prefer the limp Joyce to young men like this one, thought Patrick; but then the waiter had scarcely glanced at her. She had scant choice if no male showed any interest in her.

'He says the families here have mostly lived on the island for generations. There used to be a lot of sponge divers here, but that's died out now from Mikronisos. Synthetic sponges, you know, stealing the market, and it's a dangerous way of getting a living. The young people all want to go to Athens to get better paid work and the girls to find husbands,' said George. He spoke to the boy again and then continued, 'there are a few villas on the far side of the island. They belong to rich business-men from Athens who come in their private yachts. One man has been conducting a survey of the hinterland and plans to build a hotel if he can get permission.'

'Oh, where? *Pou einai?*' Patrick could manage that one.

The boy grinned and gestured as he answered.

'Over the hill there. Seems there's a fine beach around the coast a little way,' said George.

'Near where the accident was a few days ago?' asked Patrick.

George put the question and the boy nodded. He went away to fetch their drinks, and Patrick wondered whether to get George to ask directly for Ilena and Yannis. He decided to leave it for the moment; the day lay ahead of them.

They pottered along the water-front and into the few shops. Elsie seemed to have taken a fancy to Celia; they exclaimed together over the woven bags and embroideries. There were women in charge of all the shops, and most of them were elderly; was one of them Ilena?

A jeweller's shop attracted them, and they spent some time in its dim interior. The work was intricate, and seemed to Patrick to be ridiculously cheap. There were delicate gold earrings like those Ursula Norris had worn. Celia admired a bracelet made of fine mesh with inserts in a Greek key pattern, and Patrick bought it for her. She protested, blushing an ugly shade of crimson under her sunburn.

'A reminder of Greece, and of what I hope will be a happy day,' he said. 'Please accept it.'

She gave in, with a mumbled, somewhat graceless phrase of thanks.

'You want to be careful,' warned George as they emerged into the sunlight, Celia twisting the bracelet round her sturdy wrist. 'You'll give her ideas.'

'There's no risk of that,' said Patrick. He wondered if any man, other than her father, had given Celia a gift in her life.

'I suppose you meet all sorts of people at Oxford University,' said George.

He must visualize the university as a campus apart, as so many Americans did, Patrick thought.

'Yes. Good fits, and misfits,' said he. He was warming towards George, whose company was proving an asset to the day. And so was Elsie's: she was drawing Celia out so that the girl talked with animation, and now she suggested that Celia should visit the States on a teaching exchange for a year or two.

'I'll give you our address, and you can look us up,' said Elsie. 'Isn't that right, George?'

'What did you say, dear?'

Elsie repeated what she had just said, and Patrick walked on ahead of them. He crossed the paved area before the shops and stood on the quayside looking at the fishing boats moored in the harbour. Octopuses hung from the rigging, drying in the sun. Further along the quay men were mending nets.

As he watched the peaceful scene a dinghy with an out-board motor came slowly towards some steps leading down from the jetty beyond where the men were working; Patrick saw a female figure waiting there to be collected. The woman wore a black skirt and a white blouse, and carried a basket. The man in the boat helped her aboard, taking her basket and settling her with some care on the thwart amidships. They circled round below Patrick and he had a good look at them both. The man was Spiro's companion from Crete, the same one whom he had seen on the Acropolis the night before; the woman was grey-haired, sunburned and lined, like any Greek woman of her age, but she did not look like a peasant; there was no air of poverty about her. The dinghy, cutting a great wake as it turned, put on speed and zoomed away from the shore. Further out, at anchor in the bay, was the *Psyche;* Patrick recognized the boat by her lines, but to confirm it, as he raised his binoculars, there was the bright blonde hair of Jill as she stood on the deck waiting to help the older woman climb the awkward steps and go aboard.

VI

'Where's this beach you say is so nice, Celia?' asked George, as they walked back to the *taverna* for an early lunch. 'I was wondering if it would be an idea to get a boat to take us around there when we've eaten. We'll all feel like a snooze, I guess, and maybe a swim.'

Patrick silently blessed him. He was making it all so easy.

'We certainly can't swim here,' said Elsie, looking at the harbour. There were signs of garbage in the water, and the slight odour of primitive drainage inseparable from similar picturesque spots all over the globe.

'It's just around there,' said Celia, pointing to where the land ran out into a small promontory to form the bay, making a natural harbour. 'There won't be anyone else there, I'm certain.'

'Let's do that,' said Patrick firmly.

'You go fix lunch, then. I'll grab us a boat for later,' said George. He wandered off towards the fishermen, his expensive camera swinging from his shoulder. His clothes were typically American — the bright shirt, the narrow pale trousers — and he wore his hair cut very short, but his features, with the strongly marked brows and deepset dark eyes showed his origins. He looked more Greek each time they met, thought Patrick, and wondered what Elsie really felt about this sentimental pilgrimage.

'You speak no Greek, Mrs Loukas?' Patrick asked her, as the three of them sat down at a table beneath the straw roof that shaded the *taverna* while George talked to the fishermen.

'Say, call me Elsie, do,' she replied. 'No, just a few words like *parakalo*.' She pronounced it with a strong drawl.

'I can ask for things in shops, or where something is, but I can't understand the answers,' Celia confessed. She had not thought of Joyce for the past hour.

'You English are bad at languages, isn't that so?' said Elsie.

'We have that reputation,' said Patrick. 'Don't you think of yourself as English any more?'

'Not after all this time in the States,' replied Elsie. 'I wouldn't know my way around any more. And the language changes all the time.'

'That's true.' Idiom did alter rapidly. 'You don't speak any other languages?'

'Uh-huh.' She shook her head.

Their beer, which they had successfully ordered without George's linguistic aid, arrived, and he returned to say he had arranged for a boat to take them round the point in three-quarters of an hour.

'We don't want to sit over lunch too long,' he said.

They ordered the local speciality, a concoction of prawns and other unidentifiable fishy bits in a cheese sauce. It was rich and good. Celia ate with gusto. Afterwards she had *baclava*, while the others settled for fresh peaches. They finished with coffee. George chose the strong Greek variety; the others were given a curious mixture, very sweet and only tepid, served in a glass.

'Ugh, too sweet,' said Elsie, and left hers.

Patrick and Celia, bonded by their philhellenism, drank theirs down with false expressions of pleasure. Then it was time to meet their boatman.

He was old and grizzled, his face and hands burnt almost black from the sun, and his vessel was a shallow-draughted old boat with an engine amidships. Her name was painted on the bow in Greek characters and Celia laboriously spelled out NAFSIKA — the *Nausicaa.*

'I thought she came from Corfu,' said Celia.

'Maybe Charon here did too, and got kind of stuck,' said Elsie, eyeing their mariner dubiously. It was the first flash of wit Patrick had discerned in her; perhaps George's love-affair with this country was hard for her to tolerate. She'd become American, put the past behind her, and might not enjoy wallowing in remembered emotion.

They clambered aboard, and as they set off, fumes from the old engine filling the air, George and the boatman jabbered away happily together. Their talk was punctuated with cries of '*po, po, po,*' and excited gestures.

The *Psyche* was nowhere to be seen. She had gone round the point in the direction they were taking now soon after the elderly woman had climbed on board. There must be a lot of traffic between the islands, but it had not occurred to Patrick that Spiro would venture far from Crete. Why not, though? The *Psyche* was a sound, seaworthy vessel capable of travelling in any water.

The island, seen from the sea, looked very barren once the buildings round the harbour had disappeared. There were few trees and only sparse scrub on the grey, rocky slopes. The boatman addressed them all in the tone of a guide, and George, translating, said that there had been some volcanic eruption on the island a very long time ago destroying the thriving small community. Now some rich men dwelt on the further side, otherwise they had seen most of the population in the harbour.

'The same eruption that engulfed Crete?' asked Celia.

The boatman did not know.

'Some archaeologists were working here before the war,' he says,' George relayed to them. 'They had to stop when the war came.'

'No one's tried since?'

'Nope.'

After some consultation the boatman took them in to a wide white beach with rocks on either side of it coming down to the water. Here there were a few wispy pine trees rising from the shoreline.

'This is where you came the other day?' Patrick asked Celia, and she nodded.

The boat grounded and they took off their shoes to wade the last few yards to the shore. Celia's toes, already revealed in her sandals, were twisted, and she had a cruel bunion. Was there no end to her misfortunes? Patrick averted his eyes and took her arm in case she stumbled in the shallows; she must have been born disaster-prone.

The *Nausicaa* left them, after her captain had promised to return in time to take them back to catch the ferry.

'I hope he won't forget. I'd hate to be shipwrecked here,' said Elsie.

George and Patrick had both pressed notes into the boatman's grimy hand; he would not forget them. By this time they were all rather sleepy, and were glad to find a patch in the shade where they could rest. Elsie stripped off her dress and was revealed in a green bikini; for her age her figure was good, and very muscular; she had freckles on her back. Patrick who had brought *Phineas Finn* as well as his bathing things, spread out his towel and changed behind a rock. Then he settled down to read. With luck the others would soon fall asleep; the heat and the meal had made him feel inert and he needed to opt out of conversation for a while.

Celia staked out her small encampment further along the beach, still in the shade. She walked a long way before finding a spot that suited her for disrobing; When she returned she wore a brightly-flowered one-piece swim-suit which bulged where she did, distorting the pattern into grotesque designs. But why shouldn't she sunbathe, like everyone else? It might improve her acne. Patrick hid from the dismal spectacle behind *Phineas Finn*.

After some time they all fell asleep, but Patrick started awake almost immediately; he felt it decadent to doze during the day. He took off his glasses and walked quietly into the sea. It was warm and crystal clear, and he swam along parallel to the shore with a slow, strong stroke for quite a distance. Then he lay on his back and tried to imagine the scene on the day of Murcott's accident. Much as today; but instead of the quartet deployed on the beach there would have been thirty or so people. It would have been noisier, for they would swim or paddle, he supposed. Jeremy would have been scurrying about among them like an anxious terrier, with Joyce no doubt close on his heels and Celia brooding in the distance. Murcott had been interested in the rock formation, someone had said; so he had walked off to investigate it.

A slight movement caught his attention and he looked round to see a swimming figure approaching. The vivid colours revealed as it broke the surface told him that it was Celia. She was a fine swimmer, travelling fast through the water without splashing, her ugly face immersed. Even without his glasses, Patrick could appreciate her power.

How gratifying. Everyone could do something well, if only they were able to discover what it was, and here was Celia's talent shown.

'What a good swimmer you are,' he told her.

Overcome, she submerged briefly like a herbaceous whale, vast in her floral costume.

'I grew up by the sea,' she said. 'Near Clacton.'

'Where did the accident happen?' he asked. 'Far from the beach?'

'Not very far. I can't see without my glasses, but it's a bit to the right from where we are now. Mr Murcott was interested when he saw the volcanic evidence — it's easy to recognize here, isn't it, even if you're not a geologist? He wandered off.'

'Could you show me where he went? I'm morbidly fascinated,' Patrick said. 'Or is it too far in this heat?'

'Oh no. I'll show you,' said Celia with some eagerness.

'We'll swim again afterwards,' Patrick said. 'Race you back now.'

She won, and on her own merits.

George and Elsie had disappeared when they walked up the beach. Their towels, indented by their bodies, lay crumpled on the sand. Patrick put on dry swimming trunks and a shirt, and slung his binoculars round his neck; Celia appeared from behind her rock wearing a cyclamen-pink towelling dress. Her hair hung limply round her head in sodden strands like a travesty of Ophelia. They walked off over the sand on to the dusty ground beyond and began to climb.

'Who suggested the trip to Mikronisos. Can you remember?' asked Patrick.

Celia pondered.

'It was Mr Murcott,' she said at last. 'Yes, I'm sure it was. He'd heard about it somehow. It's not an island you do hear mentioned much.'

'No. Not like Delos, or Mykonos.'

'Or Santorin, if you're thinking about volcanoes,' said Celia. 'Mr Winterton didn't want to come. He said it was uninteresting.'

'He did join you, though?'

'Yes, he came.'

'What's his job? Do you know?'

'Mr Winterton's? He's retired, surely? Most of these people are.'

Patrick, accustomed to elderly dons who worked for ever, had forgotten this aspect of life in other professions.

They spent some time guessing what he might have done and decided that he was that vague thing, a civil servant.

'Murcott was, presumably, a geologist?'

'No, I think it was just a hobby,' said Celia.

Jeremy had been unable to supply Patrick with any of this information; he strove to keep his mind on less earthly matters and did not look in people's passports, even when they died by misadventure. Patrick, had it fallen to him to pack up the dead man's possessions, would have pried inquisitively through them wanting to know all he could about the man.

'I think he worked for a charity of some sort, raising funds,' said Celia. 'But I'm not sure.'

'You liked him.' It was a statement.

'Yes,' Celia sounded surprised. 'I suppose I did. He always said good-morning, and so on.'

Was she accustomed to being ignored most of the time? Patrick found that he could enjoy her company if he was not forced to look at her. Oh, how much the wrapping of a parcel matters, he thought. If she lost two stone and got rid of her acne, Celia's life would be transformed.

'That's where he fell.' She pointed.

A sheer cliff rose up in front of them, the stratified rock plainly revealed in the bright sunshine.

'Was he clambering up it? How unwise.'

'He must have been,' said Celia. 'I didn't see him climbing, but he was lying at the bottom. He had a stone in his hand — tightly clutched, it was — as if he'd grabbed at the rock to save himself.'

They walked over to the spot.

'Jeremy said you were splendid, coping afterwards,' said Patrick.

'Did he?' She blushed. 'That was nice of him. But you have to, don't you, when something happens?'

'Some people turn away from disaster,' he said, and added, 'I wonder what the view's like from the top. I'd like to look.'

'Oh, don't you try climbing up,' Celia besought him.

'I'm not going up that cliff, don't worry,' said Patrick. 'There may be an easier route to the top.' He scanned the hillside. Small bushes and tufts of greenery, now withered, sprouted from the rocks in places, and the slope beside the cliff looked less extreme. 'I'll look for the goat trail,' he added.

Celia stared at him in dismay.

'Oh, don't you come. It's much too hot,' he said hastily. 'Can you get back to the others? They may wonder where we are.' Patrick suspected that George had led Elsie away from the beach for some amorous dalliance; it was a pity to waste such a setting, and he wished he had come in more tempting company himself.

'All right,' She hesitated. 'Be careful.'

'I will. If I'm not back in an hour, come and look for me,' he said.

He strode off then, and Celia watched him picking out a route among the small bushes and the bare rocks, describing a traverse to the right of the sheer drop. It looked as if once the whole slope had been more gentle, and then some sort of avalanche-type fall had created the sheer face at the foot of which Dermott Murcott had lain. Surely he would have chosen the easier ascent too? She thought about it for a few minutes as she made her way back towards the beach; then basic physical distress drove everything else from her mind, for she was streaming with perspiration and her fat thighs were chafed from the friction of walking in the heat. She turned round a few times during her journey to look for Patrick, and saw his blue shirt moving gradually upwards in a slanting course on the hillside.

Patrick had found what looked like a track made by animals: a donkey trail, perhaps, or maybe his jesting remarks about goats had been, in fact, accurate. He was soon sweating; his shirt stuck to his back, but the warm sweet air was dry and clean in his lungs. He was not wearing his Cretan straw hat; he had left it on the beach, which was a pity, for he could have done with its protection from the glaring sun. His hair fell forward as he walked along, and he pushed it back impatiently. Once he stopped and surveyed the vista around him through his binoculars. There was a liner on the horizon; it gleamed white even at such a distance. Below, he could see the pink figure of Celia wending her way back to the beach.

He walked on, taking care where he stepped, for the ground was rough and stony. The light was brilliant; every dried blade of grass stood out sharp against its fellows; each wisp of withered thyme and rock-rose was crisply defined against the dry, dusty earth from which it sprang; here and there an asphodel rose, tall and spiky, the blossom delicate, the grey stem slender, miraculously sustaining the life of the bloom in its arid surroundings. A cigarette-end, thoroughly squashed, the brand name illegible, caught his eye, and he picked it up. His own sense of smell was acute, perhaps because he did not smoke himself, and he sniffed it; it was not made of Greek tobacco. Patrick wrapped it carefully in his handkerchief and put it in his shirt pocket; he saw no more alien objects during his ascent.

At last he reached the top and paused for a moment to get his breath and bearings. Nothing stirred in the limpid air. He walked on until he stood above the spot where Murcott had been found. An older man than himself, or one less fit, might, standing there after a strenuous climb, feel dizzy, faint, or have a heart attack; he might, like Felix, simply have lost his balance.

Patrick turned his back to the sea and looked inland; in front of him the ground was level for a hundred yards or more; then it rose again and formed another ridge, not a high one. He walked towards it over earth littered with small stones and shrivelled plants. At the top of it he found himself suddenly looking into a chasm; he stood on a hilly spine which rose up from the flatter land of the island like the vertebrae of some sleeping animal. He could see right across to the sea on the further side, and with his binoculars picked out the various villas the boatman had mentioned, white in the sunlight.

Suddenly, from nowhere, the figure of a woman appeared beneath him at the foot of the steep drop. She seemed to have sprung from the ground. She was walking away from him, and he focussed his binoculars on her; a moment later she disappeared again behind a rock, then reappeared mounted, on a donkey, riding away. Her face, magnified by the glasses, sprang up sharply in his vision for an instant as she turned her head; he was sure it was the woman he had seen going out with Spiro's friends towards the *Psyche* earlier in the day.

There must be a way down the cliff: he looked at his watch; was there time to climb down, investigate what lay below, and return before Celia considered him lost? Reluctantly, he decided that it could not be done; in twenty minutes she would start looking for him; he would have to return. He knew that there were caves, shepherds' refuges, and hidden spots for fugitives on all these islands. Dermott Murcott might have had time to go down the hill; if so, what had he found?

As he turned away to go back to the beach something flashed from near a rock close to where the woman had appeared with the donkey, as if the sunlight had caught against glass, mirror-like. Instinct made Patrick continue his turning movement; he walked away slowly, loitering to admire the view and betrayed no sign of having seen anything unusual. Thus, he saved his life.

Celia was alone on the beach when he reached it; she looked forlorn, and was very pleased to see him.

'I don't know where the others are,' she said. 'There hasn't been a sign of them.'

'Let's have a swim,' said Patrick. 'They'll turn up, I expect. Or don't you want to?'

Celia did. She lumbered down the beach beside him and they swam together, up and down, both from time to time peering blearily at the land but unable, without their glasses, to see anything distinctly. When they returned Elsie was sitting on the towel again, combing her hair; her bikini was quite dry. George was standing looking out to sea, smoking; his face wore an abstracted look, but his expression lightened when Patrick joined him.

George had offered round a packet of Chesterfields after lunch, but he was the only smoker among the four of them.

'Have a sweet?' Elsie offered. She took from her bag a packet of barley-sugar sweets.

'Thanks,' said Celia, taking one.

Patrick had one too; he felt the need of some quick energy.

Their boatman came for them, as promised, and when Patrick asked if there were time to circumnavigate the island before the ferry left, agreed that it could be done. They chugged along the coastline, keeping close inshore, and Patrick inspected both land and sea through his binoculars as they went. They saw the villas, three of them, where the rich Athenians lived; each had small private landing-stages running into the sea.

'They've all got yachts,' George passed on the information. One was tied up against its owner's jetty; the others were presumably cruising somewhere. They passed another boat at anchor not far from land. On deck lay a blonde girl, sunbathing; she sat up to look at them as they puttered past. She was Jill McLeod, and the boat was the *Psyche*.

VII

Celia's upper arms were lobster-red from the sun which had baked them during the trip round the island.

'You'll be sore tonight,' Elsie told her as they sat in the saloon of the ferry bound for Piraeus again, with cooling drinks before them.

Celia did not care. She wore the bracelet which Patrick had given her; it was armour against Joyce's future barbs.

'You go home tomorrow?' Patrick asked.

'Yes. In the afternoon. We're due at Gatwick about half-past six, I think.'

'BEA?'

'No — we came on a charter. *Flyways*,' she said.

Patrick nodded. He was pensive, staring into his beer. He had found neither Ilena nor Yanis, but there was some mystery connected with the island, he was convinced. And what was the Psyche doing there? He thought about Libya, the Lebanon, and Turkey: all of them easily reached by a small boat which could slip in and out unseen at night. Had not such voyages been made constantly during the war, undetected? It must be easier still now. He would not be able to return to Mikronisos himself till after his expedition to Delphi; someone, however, must be told what he had seen on the island.

But then, what had he seen? A stubbed-out cigarette-end, not Greek, possibly American or British; a woman on a donkey appearing out of nowhere; a flash of light that might have come from field-glasses or ordinary spectacles. All of these things were innocent in themselves; no one had openly threatened him, and he had seen nothing to indicate the presence of contraband or anything else suspicious.

But Desmond Murcott might have had more opportunity. And he was dead.

He asked George and Elsie what they intended to do in the next few days and learned they were bound for Delphi.

'Why, so am I,' he said. 'When do you go?'

'Tomorrow.'

'I'm going tomorrow. Perhaps we'll meet up there.'

'Say, why don't we go together?' said George. 'How did you plan to travel? On the coach?'

'I was going to hire a car,' said Patrick.

'Honey, wouldn't that be a lot more comfortable than the coach?' George said. 'Would you mind if we came along? We'd share the cost, naturally.'

Patrick tried to decide quickly whether he did mind.

'I'm not sure how long I'll be staying,' he prevaricated. 'Certainly one night; perhaps more.'

'That's O.K. If you want to come back at a different time we'll get some other transport for the return trip. We'll be staying a night too.'

Patrick made up his mind. To refuse would be churlish.

'Of course we must go together. It's a fine idea,' he said.

'You can call us at the Hilton when you've got it all fixed,' said George. 'We'll be glad to fit in with you, timewise. You'll be keeping your room in Athens while you're in Delphi?'

'Oh yes.' He might lose it altogether otherwise.

'We'll be doing that too.'

They dropped Celia off on the way in to the centre of Athens; she mumbled grateful words as she got out of the taxi. Patrick would have liked to find Jeremy and hear how his day had gone, but that would have to wait. If he went with Celia into the hotel, he knew she would cling to him like a limpet.

He got out of the taxi on the corner of Stadiou and walked down a narrow street to his own hotel while George and Elsie went on to the Hilton. Suddenly the evening stretched bleakly ahead, to be spent alone. He telephoned someone he had met before who worked at the Embassy and had a flat in Kolonaki not far away; there was no reply. He must be out of Athens for the weekend.

There was always *Phineas Finn*.

He showered, changed and shaved. Afterwards, without putting his own light on, he looked out of the window at the room across the way. It had changed occupants; a middle-aged Japanese was standing on the balcony, smoking. Patrick watched him for a few minutes while he made up his mind what to do.

At length he decided.

He picked up pencil and paper and drafted a cable to Detective-Inspector Colin Smithers at Scotland Yard. If Colin were not on duty, the wording of the message would ensure that it was passed on to him at once, or dealt with in his absence.

He put the cigarette-end he had found on the island into an envelope and sealed it securely. It might be important.

VIII

Patrick walked along Venizelou towards Omonia Square. A good dinner had revived him, and he felt drawn towards the bustling crowds in the streets. All nations mingled; tourists ambled along slowly, and citizens of Athens hurried. The traffic tore noisily by; one quickly grew used to it, he found. He sauntered along looking at the shops and the people. A plump woman telephoned from one of the tobacco and sweet kiosks on the pavement; he had noticed some fine blue telephone boxes in Constitution Square, new since his last visit, but evidently the old public telephones at the kiosks still functioned. He bought a postcard showing an *evzone* in his tasselled hat and white skirt for his nephew Andrew, and one of the Parthenon, floodlit, for Robert, his scout at Mark's, and when he reached Omonia went into the subway to write them and buy stamps. Here a sub-world existed, with tourist shops as well as a post-office and the tube station. Hundreds of people milled about: there were sailors, smartly dressed in white, from cruise liners; soldiers in their dull khaki uniform; and scores of ordinary humans intent on their own affairs. He thought the Greek girls with their glossy dark hair and enormous brown eyes were enchanting. Pity he didn't know one.

Andrew, his nephew, was four. He could pick out his own name and read a few three-letter words. Optimistically Patrick printed a message about spending a day on an island; the child would certainly read fluently soon. He wrote more mundanely to Robert, who was visiting his sister in York. The girl at the post office counter was accustomed to selling stamps to tourists and provided what he needed in silence; she looked bored and tired. Patrick emerged into the upper world again and went forward to the kerb, waiting for the lights to change before crossing the road since he had picked the wrong exit from the sub-way. He had decided to call on Jeremy.

There must be a speed limit, he supposed, as cars tore past his nose, interspersed with scooters and three-wheeled pick-ups buzzing along like maddened wasps; buses lumbered by; and the pedestrians waited meekly for their turn. Patrick was not sure if jay-walking was a definite offence here; it was certainly an invitation to death.

He had barely formed this thought when something caught him between the shoulder-blades and he found himself pitching outwards in the path of a blue local bus.

Patrick was not elderly nor frail; he was very fit, with swift reflexes. He could not save himself from lurching into the road but he did not fall; he flailed at the air with his arms and at the same time somehow spun round on his heel towards the pavement; someone beside him grabbed him too, and helped to pull him back. He felt the side of the bus knock his elbow; that was all.

'*Po, po, po,*' said the stout woman who had seized him and burst into excited speech.

'*Ime Anglos. Den katalaveno*' said Patrick, with surprising calm under the circumstances. '*Efkaristo poli,*' he added. 'Thank you very, very much.'

'You are O.K.?'

'Yes, yes.' What a fool the woman must think him, falling about like that. He thanked her again, allowed her to shepherd him over the road when the traffic halted, and parted from her only after they had warmly shaken hands.

He had been pushed. There was no doubt in his mind. A hand had definitely been placed on his back and he had been shoved towards the oncoming bus. Only luck had saved him from serious injury.

He walked on very thoughtfully towards the Livingstone Hotel, taking care to keep well away from other pedestrians at the lesser roads he had to cross on the way.

There was no sign of Jeremy or any of his group in the bar or any of the public rooms. They might have gone out for a last look at the city by night; or they might be up on the roof.

He took the lift to the roof garden, and stepped from it on to a concrete floor and the sound of throbbing machinery which he realized was the air-conditioning plant. A smell of cooking came from a vent as he walked past it, on his way towards a group of people standing at the roof edge looking out over the city. He recognized none of them, so he moved on over the large area of roof, past the bar, now closed, until he came to the pool. The surface of the water glittered with an oily sheen; a liberal dilution with sun-tan oil. Two people sat beside it, holding hands and murmuring.

Far away out at sea the lights of the American Sixth Fleet shone brilliantly; a fresh breeze blew up here, and the traffic sounds were muted. Patrick avoided the edge of the roof; his assailant might have followed him up here so why make things too easy?

He went back to the hotel foyer where he asked the clerk to ring Jeremy's room. There was no reply, so he left a note asking Jeremy to call him when he got in. Then he went by taxi back to his own hotel; somehow he did not feel like walking around the city any more that night. He took a bottle of the duty-free whisky he had bought at Heathrow out of his cupboard and poured himself a stiff tot. After that he settled down with *Phineas Finn*. He was seldom so slow with a novel, but there had been so many distractions.

Jeremy thumped on his bedroom door at midnight.

IX

'Women are the devil, aren't they?' Jeremy said. 'What do you do about it?'

He sat in the only chair, a toothglass containing a generous tot of whisky between his hands, staring glumly at the small strip of carpet on the floor. Patrick was perched on the side of the bed. It was not an encouraging setting for a confessional, if that was what was to come, but it would have to do.

'In what way do you mean?' asked Patrick cautiously. He thought of Ellen. My God, I scarcely knew her, he realized in an instant of revelation. What am I doing, all this time afterwards, still carrying a torch for her? He looked more kindly on his former pupil, whose sudden remark had illumined his own folly.

'Well,' Jeremy hesitated, self-conscious but determined. Patrick, after all, had been his tutor. 'I don't have much of a problem myself, if you know what I mean. But they get at me.'

Could he really have no sexual drive? Patrick regarded him with interest. It was sad; not a matter for envy. Better the torment.

'Joyce?' he prompted.

'She's like a limpet — or — or an octopus,' said Jeremy, and shuddered.

'What's happened?'

'Well—' Jeremy seemed unable to say.

'Start at the beginning,' Patrick advised. 'I've no idea how the day went. You managed the funeral all right, I suppose?'

'Yes — oh yes. It went off very well,' said Jeremy. 'It seems ages ago, in fact. I'd almost forgotten about it.'

'Everyone came? Except Celia?'

'Yes. A few opted out of the graveside bit, thank goodness. It was very hot.'

'Arthur Winterton was there?'

'Yes.' Jeremy looked surprised at the idea that he might not have been present.

'What happened afterwards?'

'Most of the group went off for coffee in Constitution Square. Arthur Winterton didn't, as a matter of fact. He went to the Benaki Museum.'

'Alone?'

'Yes — yes, I'm sure he went alone.'

'And after coffee?'

'Oh — well, then everyone went back to the hotel, and we had lunch, and then we went to a beach near Vouliagmeni for a swim. We'd hired a coach.'

'They're keen swimmers, are they, your troop?'

'Well — not really. A few, perhaps. Some just paddled. I'm not much of a swimmer myself but I like it when it's warm.'

Patrick could imagine him standing skinny in the shallows, encouraging the older people. He was good with them, and they liked him. How did he manage with the very young? He had always been rather an odd-man-out among his peers though their inevitable teasing had seldom been malicious.

'I couldn't shake Joyce off,' he sighed. She'd kept touching him. At first he thought it accidental, but it happened too often for that, and in the bus she'd sat next to him, her thin leg tight against his thigh. 'She's not even pretty,' he burst out.

'She couldn't have got up to much in Vouliagmeni, with everybody there,' Patrick said mildly.

'Well, to be fair, she was a help in some ways,' Jeremy calmed down enough to swallow some whisky. 'She ran around seeing everyone was all right, getting refreshments — the quantity of lemonade and tea we've consumed this trip would fill a lake. One's always thirsty in this heat. And this evening we did a tour of Athens by Night. It wasn't bad — most of them enjoyed it. Bouzouki music and all that. It was a good thing, really, after such a sad morning.'

'That can't be what upset you, Jeremy,' said Patrick. 'What else happened? Did Joyce try to seduce you when you got back?'

'How did you know?' Jeremy gaped at him.

'My lightning intuition,' Patrick said.

Jeremy saw he meant it as a joke, so he smiled, but doubtfully.

'That's better. Cheer up. I'm sure you didn't fall,' said Patrick. It might have been better if he had.

'It was awful. Most embarrassing,' said Jeremy.

'How did she get you alone?'

'I've got a room to myself. I was sharing with Murcott, you see. Most of us are in doubles, it's much cheaper. She followed me in after we got back from our tour of the city. First we talked. I really thought she wanted my advice. I must be very stupid.'

Patrick thought that he was, on the contrary, one of life's few genuine innocents. But was he, in fact, quite adult? Wasn't loss of innocence a necessary step in attaining maturity? He slotted the question away in his mind for future thought and turned his attention towards the earnest young man.

'She was so wet and slobbery,' Jeremy burst out. Joyce had sprung at him, fastened tentacle arms around his neck and pressed hot moist lips against his mouth. Then her tongue. Jeremy shuddered again at the memory.

'She can't have raped you. What did you do?'

'I didn't want to hurt her feelings,' said Jeremy. It had been physically extremely difficult to disentangle himself from

Joyce's clinging limbs; she seemed to be all over him and she was just as strong as he was. After a while, when he thought he must soon suffocate, she had removed her avid mouth from his unresponsive lips and burst into verbal praise of his patience and goodness. This had given him a chance to break free; he had thrust her away and grabbed a chair to put between them.

'Then I ran away. For all I know she's still there,' said Jeremy. 'I daren't go back.'

Patrick poured them both some more whisky.

'Where was Celia during all this?'

'Goodness knows. She keeps a sharp eye on Joyce as a rule, but of course she wasn't at Vouliagmeni. She was with you.'

'But she came on your trip round the night spots?'

'Yes.' She'd sat with Gareth Hodgson on the coach and sent dagger looks at Joyce throughout the evening. 'She had a good day with you,' Jeremy added. 'She said that it was wonderful.' She'd shown off her bracelet proudly. 'You were kind to her.'

'I was making use of her,' said Patrick bluntly. 'I wanted to see where Murcott's accident happened. And I was sorry for her. She was crucifying herself with jealousy over Joyce.'

Jeremy tried to look broad-minded.

'She can't help being what she is,' he said, but he primmed his lips.

'I'm not convinced that she is what you think she is,' said Patrick. 'She hasn't a chance of a relationship with a man; she'd probably be terrified if she had. So her emotions have never passed the schoolgirl stage. Even hideous people have sexual desires.'

'Oh, I know,' Jeremy acknowledged it in the same way as he would have acknowledged the existence of any biological function; you did not have to understand it to accept that it was there.

'It can be tragic,' Patrick added.

'What's the answer?'

'You're the parson. You tell me.'

'I don't understand these things,' Jeremy admitted. 'I suppose I lack something or other.' Perhaps he did; some hormone, possibly. 'I like girls, you know, if they're good sports.' He had kissed one or two, chastely, to see what it was like. It had made him tingle slightly, nothing more; perhaps he did not go about it in the right way. But he had thought that Joyce was about to devour him.

'You manage. And women like you,' Jeremy continued, this time in accusing tones. He had often seen Patrick, in Oxford, with various females, usually rather attractive ones. 'But you're not married.'

'Well, no. It hasn't worked out, one way and the other,' said Patrick drily. 'It's all very difficult. Marriage is so permanent.' And involved such a commitment. But sometimes he hungered for a mutually renewing relationship; it could mean an end to restlessness. 'I'm not as high-minded as you are, Jeremy,' he added lightly. 'I give in to temptation quite easily.'

'You wouldn't have given in to Joyce.'

'Well, no. I doubt if I'd have found it tempting,' said Patrick gravely. But he must not be flippant; Jeremy required practical guidance. 'Don't get yourself into corners alone with predatory females, Jeremy. Some women go for men just because they're parsons, you know. It's an occupational hazard that goes with the cloth. I suspect you have a gift for celibacy, but even so you'll be a prey for these ladies. You'll have to acquire a defensive technique. Be ready for them. Never sit on a sofa with a girl unless you want to start something.'

Jeremy listened to this advice in amazement.

'You may meet some nice girl, one day that you'll fall for,' Patrick said, more gently. He might; some quiet, domesticated girl who would not frighten him: he would be so lonely otherwise.

'But what am I to do now?' wailed Jeremy. 'I can't go back to the hotel. She may still be there.

'I'll ring up Celia,' said Patrick, and reached out for the telephone.

'What — at this hour?'

'Yes. If Joyce has gone back to their room they'll be having a row; and if she hasn't, Celia will be awake like the mother of a wayward child. Do you know the number of their room?'

Jeremy did.

In a few minutes Patrick was talking to Celia. Joyce was not in their room and she was frantic, but she knew where she was.

'Jeremy's here, with me,' said Patrick, and heard the distraught breathing at the other end of the line grow quieter.

'Can you get her out?'

'Yes,' said Celia. 'It's happened before.' Her voice was calmer. 'They don't always run away,' she added.

Probably not.

'You'll soon be safe, Jeremy,' said Patrick. 'Now, give Celia ten minutes or so to cope, and then it will be clear for you to go back. Tell me about Arthur Winterton meanwhile.'

But Jeremy knew very little about him.

'He's very deaf — wears a hearing-aid — hadn't you noticed? He's retired — a widower, I think. He didn't come with us to Vouliagmeni this afternoon, by the way. I don't know anything else about him. Why do you ask?'

'No reason. I'm just incurably nosy,' said Patrick cheerfully. 'Does he smoke?'

'Yes,' said Jeremy.

PART FOUR:
SUNDAY AND MONDAY

DELPHI AND ATHENS

I

Early next morning George Loukas telephoned to discuss when they would leave for Delphi. Elsie was tired, he said, and wanted to lie-in for a while. Would eleven o'clock suit Pattrick?

This was what happened when you contracted to do things with other people. Patrick sighed inwardly; he wanted to get on with the day. But he agreed with fair grace, and dawdled about packing the few things he would need for a night or two in the mountains, trying not to feel irritable.

At half past eight Jeremy rang to apologize for his conduct the night before.

'I ought to have coped without bothering you,' he said.

'My dear chap, don't give it a thought,' said Patrick. 'Was everything all right?'

'Yes. Joyce had gone when I got back. And she didn't appear at breakfast. Celia said she had it in bed.'

'Very wise. Well, after today you need never see her again.'

Feeling himself to be the ultimate in hypocrites, Patrick wished Jeremy a good trip back. Colin had cabled saying: STEPS WILL BE TAKEN. A nice reception would therefore be waiting for the party when they reached Gatwick. As for himself, perhaps it was as well he was leaving Athens for a time; he did not want to be the victim of another accident. He was still unsure of his own propriety: instead of cabling Colin, perhaps he ought to have told the Greek police about Arthur Winterton; the smuggling of narcotics was one of the most serious crimes in the book, and how better to do it than in the baggage of a seemingly inoffensive elderly tourist? Pounds of the stuff could get in that way, dispersed through various groups. But the matter might have a totally innocent explanation; Arthur Winterton might have been collecting a book or some other harmless object that night.

Celia telephoned next. She wanted to thank him for everything, she said, sounding tearful.

Patrick demurred; he needed no thanks.

'Oh, but I had such a lovely day yesterday. And the bracelet. And then last night; you were so kind.'

'You managed.'

'Yes.' There was no need to describe the abuse Joyce had hurled at her. In the end Celia had made her swallow a sleeping pill. 'She'll be all right. It'll be forgotten.' After days of punitive silence.

'Good luck,' said Patrick. He managed to fight down an impulse to ask her to call on him at Mark's if she were ever in Oxford.

'I'm going to think seriously about Elsie Loukas's idea of going to America,' Celia said earnestly.

'You do that.' The climate might suit her better, or the charms of her British accent outweigh her lack of other allure. Anyway, a change could only do good.

'I hope you enjoy the rest of your holiday.'

'I'm sure I will. I'm going to Delphi today.'

'Oh. I mustn't keep you, then.' She sounded wistful. They did not leave until after an early lunch so perhaps she had hoped for another meeting.

'Goodbye,' said Patrick firmly.

Sadly, Celia hung up. He pictured her grimly facing the silent Joyce. Before anyone else could get at him, he went out.

There was time to visit the Acropolis again before he picked up the car.

He walked swiftly through the busy streets, past the shoe-shine men and the people in neat clothes going to church, keeping a look-out in case anyone seemed to be trailing him; it felt slightly ridiculous, as though he were in some gangster film, but at least he could keep a physical gap between himself and anyone following him.

There were only a few people up on the great citadel so early. The breeze was fresh, and the sun not yet at its zenith. It was a good time to come. He sat down on a slab of marble well away from any slope or step, so that no one could approach him unseen, and began to think about Felix.

Suicide. Could Inspector Manolakis's suspicions, unvoiced though they were, be right?

Felix was an able scholar, much respected even if not among the top flight in his field. He had published numerous papers and two books on Roman History, and was preparing another. Surely he would never kill himself with an unfinished job like that on his hands?

What else did he know about Felix? There was his weakness about heights, and his limp. He'd been in the army during the war and was captured in the Western desert. He had been wounded in the leg and had spent some time in a German field hospital before being sent to a prisoner-of-war camp in Germany where he had remained until the war ended. Patrick had never heard him talk much about those days; he seemed to remember some vague rumour that Felix had escaped from the camp once, but had been recaptured very quickly, and that someone who had escaped with him was shot, but Patrick was uncertain if that was in fact just what had happened. Could some sort of delayed, suppressed depression have caught up with him now? If so, why go to Crete to indulge it? He could have thrown himself over the side of the *Persephone* equally well. It didn't make sense. No, either it was an accident, however hard to explain, or it was something much more sinister.

His elbow felt bruised this morning.

He thought back to the evening before and the feel of that hand in his back. He hadn't imagined it. But either the pusher had lost his nerve or the attempt had been meant merely to incapacitate, not to kill, for these people were experts: their accidents ended in fatalities.

It was time to go.

He walked carefully back into the city, but no one came near him.

II

They drove through the suburbs of Athens, along wide streets with large houses set in shady gardens on either side; then past factories and new buildings until they joined the motorway. The car, another Fiat, was almost new; it was more powerful than the one Patrick had hired in Crete, and he enjoyed driving this one. Elsie sat in front beside him while George read the map in the back. At intervals Elsie handed round boiled sweets, of which she seemed to have an unlimited supply in her bag.

George pointed out the plain of Marathon, and said they must remember to watch for the spot where Oedipus slew his father. After they left the motorway, just before Thebes, the road ran through miles of fertile plain before climbing into the mountains. There was not enough traffic to worry them; the tourist buses had left Athens much earlier. The Loukases had brought a picnic; they ate cold chicken, cheese and fruit, and drank rather warm beer in a shady spot where the scent of thyme filled the air. Up here it was cooler, and when they had eaten George wandered off with his camera. He took film of Elsie and Patrick sitting under an olive tree and then strolled down the road to capture shots of the plain below.

Elsie packed up the remains of the picnic; her movements were neat and economical. She seemed relaxed today; perhaps the magic of Greece had reached her at last. The unexpected visit to Crete must have been a traumatic experience for her when the island held such associations from the past.

They talked in a desultory fashion. Patrick told Elsie about Alec Mudie and their plan to travel together. A thought came to him, and he said, 'I wonder if you ever met Alec?'

Elsie repeated his name and said, consideringly, 'I don't think so. Why should I have done?'

'He served in Crete. So did your first husband, I believe,' said Patrick.

'They may have met. Freddie was killed in 1941,' said Elsie.

'Oh — in the battle. Alec didn't get there till later,' said Patrick. 'He was landed by submarine. He was a classical scholar who spoke only ancient Greek in those days. An unconventional sort of soldier.'

'So was Freddie. He was an archaeologist,' Elsie said.

'You shared his interest?' She had not seemed much stirred by what she had seen so far.

'Not really. There wasn't time to learn much about it. He was killed a few weeks after we married,' she said. 'We met at a dance, not on a dig.'

George returned to them then, and Patrick dropped the subject. He had been tactless, perhaps, to raise it, but she had not seemed to mind. The car had cooled down in the shade where they had parked, and they resumed their journey in good spirits.

In Arakhova they stopped again and walked along the street looking in the shops. George and Elsie went shopping for souvenirs while Patrick ambled about, content to admire the grandeur of his surroundings and the little village perched on the side of the mountain. The commercial exploitation of the place did not worry him at all; Delphi, in the days when the oracle spoke, must have been a mecca for tourism. The more people who came to see for themselves the beauty of its setting, the better, he thought, and why shouldn't they carry away with them mementoes of their visit?

At the sight of the slender columns of the Tholos rising from the slopes as they approached he felt his throat tighten. Even George was mute, and as Patrick slowed the car to a halt and looked round he saw that there were tears in the other man's eyes.

'Will you look at all those coaches?' said Elsie, not awed at all.

Someone — Jeremy perhaps, in one of his informative chats — had told Patrick that two hundred coaches a day came to Delphi during the season. It was probably true. Certainly at this moment a long line of them was drawn up outside the sanctuary; more would be in the town and at the hotels.

'Let's stop for a quick look now. Then we can check in at the hotel and come on back after the crowds have gone,' suggested George.

The others agreed. Patrick found somewhere to park and they entered through the gate in the mesh fence. The afternoon sun beat down upon them, and the crowds with their guide-books and cameras moved along the Sacred Way like ants, but they did not detract from the magnificence of the setting. On such a day, in such a place, it was good indeed to be alive.

And Felix should be living, drawing nearer hour by hour aboard the *Persephone*.

They walked up as far as the theatre. A youth wearing no shirt was taking a photograph of his friend, who wore none either. Patrick saw a tourist policeman come up to reprove them both and ask them to dress. With gestures they explained they had brought no shirts with them. The policeman gave up. Odd consistency of the regime: the ancient Greeks had disported here naked in the stadium.

Their hotel was beyond the town of Delphi, built into the mountain-side overlooking the ravine with a view across the

Bay of Corinth. The huge, stone-flagged lounge was blessedly cool after the heat outside. George and Elsie went off in one direction to their room, which was in an annexe across the garden, and Patrick in another to his, a small single one at the back of the building with wide windows opening to a view of the peaks above.

He unpacked his bag, had a quick wash, and then took the car to the upper entrance to the sanctuary, above the stadium. It was seldom crowded up here; the daily coach trips from Athens allowed scant time for the whole ascent except for the nimble, who might manage a swift dash up and down again in the intervals between their guide's discourse and the moment for departure. Some visitors did not even know of the stadium's existence.

He walked along the shady, wooded path until he came to the great blocks of stone marking the perimeter of the stadium, and climbed up until he could enter it. Then he sat down, with the huge arena spread before him. A few people sat scattered about, and others strolled on the dry ground where the athletes had competed. He stayed there for about half an hour, thinking of very little except that there was some healing presence in the air; when he went back to the car he felt soothed, and more peaceful than at any time for months. A week in this place would be therapeutic.

The hotel was seething with activity when he returned to it. One small, elderly porter and a boy who looked only about twelve years old were loading enormous suitcases into an American Express coach that was about to leave. The travellers boarding it all wore their names pinned to their lapels; they were members of some confederation, and were off to Beirut after spending the night in Athens. In two weeks they would have 'done' Europe and the Middle East, Patrick heard one say.

He watched the two porters plod back and forth with the luggage; they had no trolley, and the cases were much heavier than those normally associated with air travel. Tonight more porters would unload them and take them to their rooms; in the morning it would all be done again. Patrick wondered how many coachloads changed over each night in this hotel and how many cases the man and the boy carried each day.

He shaved and showered, trying not to make too much mess; he had never yet found a Greek shower equipped with a curtain. Later, cool and refreshed, he went out on to the terrace with a drink and *Martin Chuzzlewit*. Another coach had arrived while he was in his room and the reception desk was surrounded by tired travellers; the porters were quietly bringing the cases in and lining them up in a row until the rooms had been assigned.

He sat outside, with the faint sounds of the new arrivals floating out to him from the hotel, and before him the view to the sea.

Somewhere over there the *Persephone* was steadily surging on towards Itea. Would anyone aboard her know why Felix had gone to Crete?

III

George and Elsie had not appeared by the time Patrick was ready for another drink. He wandered in to the bar to fetch it himself, as the waiter looking after the lounge and the terrace was scurrying about in a non-stop endeavour to serve other people. Still another coach had arrived; the little old porter and the boy were ferrying in more luggage. The old man's shoulders sagged under the weight of the cases he carried; the boy tried proudly not to totter with his.

Patrick saw George and Elsie walking up through the garden when he returned to the terrace; she wore a white dress gaily patterned in reds and blues, which stood out among the bushes in the grounds, and George, at her side, carried her stole in case it grew cold later.

Patrick mentioned the coach arrivals and the burdened porters. George had talked to the boy when he took their bags out to the annexe. He was twelve and had finished with school; he was proud to count as a man.

'Wish we could take him home with us and give him some more schooling,' said George.

They were joined at their table for dinner by two women who were on a tour of the classical sites by coach. It soon became clear that the two, who had never met before the tour began, were completely exhausted. They had soaked up the atmosphere of Ancient Greece with deep appreciation but were so tired that they feared they had not absorbed all they should.

'All the ruins are on the sides of mountains,' said the elder lady. 'You need to be a mountain goat to get to them.'

'You see a lot in a very short time,' said the second, who was about Patrick's age.

'The next time I come to Greece I'm going to collapse on a remote island and go nowhere,' said the other.

'We certainly are lucky being able to take time over our trip,' George said.

They had all agreed that you must make the best use of what time you had, when a sixth person joined their table. It was the cottage loaf-shaped woman who had travelled out on Patrick's flight from London the week before. He recognized her at once, though her face was now the regulation holiday pink hue; she needed reminding about where they had met; during the frisking process at Heathrow. Her name was Vera Hastings.

She was visiting Delphi alone, since her daughter had two small children too young to come.

'You must be having a great visit with them, Mrs Hastings,' said George, beaming at her. He had insisted that all the ladies share the Demestica he was providing with the meal.

Mrs Hastings was loving every minute, though it was very hot, and the noise of the planes at Glyfada, where her daughter had a flat, was excessive. She thought one grew used to it, however; Eleanor seemed scarcely to notice it now and the little boy enjoyed identifying the various airlines represented as the planes came low overhead. Under George's friendly interest, Mrs Hastings, who had seemed shy at first, soon thawed. While she talked to the Loukases, Patrick asked the other two women about their classical tour. The wine, combined with fatigue and too much concentrated culture, had gone to their heads, and they cast discretion to the winds, pointing out their companions who were distributed about the restaurant at other tables. There was one very old lady, aged eighty-four, who weighed about fifteen stone. Her iron-grey hair was swept severely back and bound with a snood; her complexion was brick red. Beside her sat a pale, meek man of about fifty-five.

'He's her son. She's very lame, and she can't climb any of the steps or precipices we have to tackle daily,' said the younger woman. 'Her son stays with her in the coach at every stop.'

'Good heavens. Why have they come?'

'I can't imagine. You'd think mama would let him off, at least, to see what they've travelled all this way for,' said the older woman. 'They live in Tunbridge Wells.'

Patrick stared at the pair, amazed.

'I've met men like that before,' said the younger woman. 'There are plenty about.'

Patrick had too. What happened when their mothers died and at last they were cast adrift?

The two women, who had started their meal before Patrick and the others, finished first, and left, apologizing. They were too tired to stay up a minute longer and intended to collapse instantly into their beds.

'Nice ladies,' said George, when they had gone. 'Widows, I suppose.' Both had worn wedding rings. 'It's sad, isn't it, to see so many lonely ladies?'

'They didn't seem particularly lonely,' said Patrick. 'They're enjoying their trip, even if they are tired.'

'I know. But what a pity.' George looked at Elsie, who was talking to Mrs Hastings. 'They're brave, of course. So was Elsie, when we met.'

'Where did you meet?'

'In Seattle. I was there on a business trip and got tooth-ache. She was the dentist's nurse.'

Elsie was telling Vera Hastings that although she was British, she had not been back to England since the war and would not know it now. She was an American citizen, naturally, after living so long in the States.

'But we're going there this trip,' said George. 'We're going to see Elsie's home town.'

'Where was that?' asked Vera.

'Reading,' said Elsie.

'Oh, I know Reading well,' said Vera. 'I don't live far away.' She named her small Berkshire town, which Elsie did not remember.

'I went abroad with the forces as soon as I was old enough,' Elsie said. 'I was married in North Africa.'

'How exciting,' Vera said. 'Were you in the A.T.S.?'

'No. The Navy.'

'She was sent back to England after her husband was killed, weren't you, honey?' George said.

'Mm. I went kind of crazy after that,' Elsie said. 'I deserted. Then I found I was pregnant — but my baby died, so I was afraid of being picked up and court-martialled.'

'Surely no court-martial would have been very hard on you?' Patrick said.

Vera seemed about to speak, but Elsie got in first.

'I guess not, but when you're young you don't understand these things,' she said, and laughed. 'What a shady past.'

'I'm sure we've all done things we're not very proud of,' Vera said, looking at Elsie in a considering way.

'What are everyone's plans for tomorrow?' George asked, seizing a chance to change the subject. He had looked uncomfortable during Elsie's moment of self-revelation.

Patrick intended to keep his plans to himself.

'I've got a date,' he said, mysteriously.

'That's all right,' said George. 'We'll be happy looking around.'

'I'm longing to see the Charioteer,' said Elsie. It was the first remark she had made that one would expect from an archaeologist's widow; even if she had not been old enough to have developed a knowledge of the subject before her husband

130

was killed, it might have followed later. But perhaps that was sentimental, Patrick told himself: the man was dead, and the girl looked ahead, not backwards.

The four had coffee together on the terrace. Then George and Elsie said they would like to go for a stroll. Vera said she was too tired to go with them.

'I feel rather like those women we met at dinner,' she confessed. 'I'll sit here for a bit, then go to bed. I haven't worn as well as you, Elsie, and we must be much the same age. I was in the Wrens too.'

'Were you? Where did you serve?' asked Elsie.

'Oh, I didn't go abroad. I was in Scotland for most of the time,' said Vera.

'Oh. Then we wouldn't have met,' said Elsie.

She and George went off, arm in arm, for their stroll, and when they had gone Patrick asked Vera if she were really content just to sit, or would she like to go for a drive?

She was too tired to stir, she said, but he must go.

'I'm tired too,' Patrick said, not altogether truthfully. He felt no urge to move; it was pleasant and cool, looking out over the mountain-side towards the Bay of Corinth and the lights that now twinkled in the distance.

'How old are your grandchildren?' he asked.

Out came the photographs then, and he learned about Eleanor, now twenty-six, and her elder brother, an accountant in Manchester. Eleanor and her family would be in Greece for three years; then the company would send them somewhere else.

'It's wonderful having this trip,' said Vera. 'The family paid; otherwise I couldn't have done it.'

Her husband, she told him, had died when both the children were quite young; she had obviously had a difficult life. She worked in a bank in the small country town where she lived.

Patrick asked her if she knew how to get to the stadium by the upper path. She didn't, so he arranged to take her there

131

in the car as soon as it opened in the morning, which was at half-past nine. She could then walk slowly through the sanctuary in a downhill direction, which would save her a lot of exertion. He could not, he said, promise to bring her back to the hotel from the lower gate or the museum, but she could probably catch a bus, or certainly take a taxi. She accepted gratefully and they arranged to meet after breakfast. She got up and said goodnight, then seemed about to say something else, but changed her mind.

When she had gone off to her room Patrick strolled alone in the garden. This was an awesome place. All that had happened here had left its mark in the atmosphere, but it was not horrific; mystic, rather.

Why was he meeting so many solitary ladies? There was Mrs Hastings and poor Celia; even Ursula Norris was alone.

Why was none of them a luscious but lonely blonde girl?

IV

Patrick had breakfast early and went for a walk. He could not bear to stay near the hotel where already the porters were starting to line up the baggage for the morning's departures; at any minute he would be helping them. The two women he had met at dinner were in the dining room, and he learned that they were returning to Athens this morning, with a stop on the way at Ossios Loukas. Then they were going to Rhodes.

The *Persephone* would soon be arriving off Itea. He had decided against meeting her when she docked; it would make a production of his encounter with the ship, when he wanted it to seem mere accident. He had met some of the other lecturers more than once; his plan was to intercept the party and express surprise at the coincidence of their being in Delphi together.

The sky was again as blue as a harebell; just a few tiny wisps of cloud scudded across. The mountain air was fresh and invigorating at that hour, before the sun rose high. When he got back to the hotel Vera Hastings was waiting for him and the two porters were mercifully absent. Long lines of suitcases, neatly stacked, showed part of their Herculean labour accomplished.

'You'll have the stadium to yourself,' Patrick said as they went out to the car.

'It's nice of you to take me,' said Vera. She looked rested, and said she had slept well. It was good to escape from the heat of Athens.

'Not at all. I'd like to come with you, but I've got to be down by the museum fairly promptly,' said Patrick.

They soon reached the upper gate. The young man selling tickets remembered Patrick from the evening before, when they had exchanged a few words of goodwill in mixed languages, with the aid of Patrick's phrase book. Patrick explained to Vera that if she kept straight on along the woodland path before her she would eventually reach the stadium, and promised to look out for her below, later on. He told her that there was a *taverna* across the road beyond the Castelian Spring, at the start of the route to the Tholos, and looked at her shoes. They were sensible canvas ones, with rubber soles.

'It's worth going down there,' he said, 'But the path's a bit rough.'

She was grateful for his advice, and they parted.

Patrick drove straight round, through the town, and down to the main entrance of the sanctuary. When he had parked the car he walked back to the museum and sat under a tree to wait till the passengers from the *Persephone* arrived. They would surely begin at the museum, he thought.

Elsie and George went past in a taxi. They did not see him under his tree. He watched them go through the entrance gates to the sanctuary and start to climb upwards. Then two large coaches arrived with stickers marked S.S. PERSEPHONE plastered across their windscreens. They stopped quite near him and the passengers emerged.

Most were elderly; a few were middle-aged. It was an expensive cruise, the sort of holiday couples raising families could not afford. As Patrick had anticipated, they assembled outside the museum and then trooped through the doors in an orderly file. Patrick tagged on at the rear. Luck was with him, for the man who seemed to be in charge was Giles Marlow, an ancient historian from Cambridge with whom Felix had carried on an amicable postal war over their differing views on some Persian finds. Patrick had met him with Felix on various occasions; the two had liked and respected each other, he knew.

Marlow's flock was well drilled. Everyone knew what to look for, presumably because Giles had lectured on the museum and its contents the evening before. They went round at a brisk pace, observing the most notable objects on display. Patrick benefited from this selective tour himself. They all ended up in an awed semi-circle around the Charioteer. He was a strangely moving figure, the broken reins in his outstretched hand, his eyes with their intent gaze seeming to be alive.

Marlow had noticed Patrick earlier. Now, with his immediate duty over, he left his charges and greeted him.

'Hope you didn't mind me latching on to listen to you,' Patrick said.

'Not a bit — I'm flattered,' said Marlow. 'What a surprise to find you here.'

'Indeed,' said Patrick mildly.

Marlow glanced at his watch.

'Sorry — our schedule's a bit tight and we're off to the sanctuary now,' he said. 'Coming?'

'Yes,' said Patrick.

Marlow addressed his followers and they all moved out into the sunshine where they set off down the road at a sedate pace. The sun was high now and the heat struck them fiercely.

'What an impressive place this is,' said Patrick.

'It is, indeed. I come here twice a year and I find it more awesome every time,' said Marlow. 'You heard about Lomax? A terrible business — he fell off some cliff in Crete. He should have been with us now.'

'Yes, it was shocking. Why did he leave you?'

'I can't tell you. Opted out in Venice. We'd only just joined the ship, in fact. Said something unexpected had cropped up and he couldn't come. I thought he'd gone home — someone ill, I imagined. Though one can't imagine Gwenda ailing.'

'Even she must have a weakness,' Patrick suggested.

'Mm. But it can't have been that, since he went to Crete.'

'Did he seem himself? Not disturbed?'

'Agitated, because he was changing his plans. Not out of his mind, if that's what you mean,' said Marlow.

'Have you replaced him?'

'No. It was too late to find someone else. We're doing his bits between us. Italy's his speciality — he'd have come into his own on our final leg. We go to Syracuse next. He said he'd be back by then. I suppose he did go off his rocker, in fact, jumping over that cliff?'

'I doubt it,' said Patrick. 'The police said it was an accident. I found his body.'

'Good God! I didn't know that!'

'No. Luckily there was almost no commotion at the time. It was all managed very discreetly,' said Patrick.

'Nasty for you.'

'Very.'

'Staying here long?'

'I'm not sure. It depends.'

'Doing a bit of a tour, are you? If you were in Crete, last week?'

'You could say that.'

Things that Felix had told him about Patrick were coming back to Marlow's mind. There was that funny business in Athens the year before; some old lady was involved.

'An astute chap,' Felix had called Patrick. High praise, in his terms.

Marlow took Patrick's elbow and edged him a little apart from the nearest *Persephone* passengers, who were clearly bursting to talk to their erudite guide but too polite to interrupt.

'Something odd must have happened. It's been very much on my mind, but there seemed to be nothing one could do about it. Too nebulous,' said Marlow. 'Men like Felix don't toss aside plans made months before for a whim. Either he was unhinged, or something important happened. There's a Mrs Amberley. Lucy. Ever heard of her?'

'No.'

'She always comes on these cruises when Lomax does — did. I've been on the same cruise myself five times. She's here now — in Delphi. She didn't come to the museum. We dropped her off in the town. She said she wanted to go up to the stadium. We don't all go there — it's such a climb, only the energetic try it. She's been there lots of times, of course. She's pretty depressed. One hasn't known quite what to say to her. He could have been fleeing from her. But she's a charming woman. And there's Gwenda—' he looked at Patrick thoughtfully.

'I'll go and look for her,' said Patrick at once.

'My dear chap. There'll be hundreds of people up there now.'

'Not in the stadium. I'll find her. What does she look like?'

The other thought.

'Smallish,' he said at last. 'Nothing special about her. Fairish hair, going grey. Forty-ish. Pleasant-looking,' he added.

'Wearing what?'

'Oh, goodness. Sort of bluey-mauve — like lavender. It matches her eyes. I noticed that,' said Marlow, inspired. 'And a hat, a straw affair.' He looked at Patrick sharply. 'You're not satisfied that Lomax died by accident?'

'Not really. It seemed a bit improbable.'

'I agree. He was a cautious sort of chap. And he'd that limp. He had to be careful clambering about. Not keen on heights, either. Noticed it at Sounion, once; he tried to hide it, but he didn't like admiring the temple with the cliff at the back of him. And suicide—' he shook his head. 'It doesn't fit. Not like that, anyway.'

'No,' said Patrick. 'I don't think it does.'

Marlow frowned.

'You go in for this kind of thing, don't you? Sorting things out.'

'It's worked out that way, once or twice.'

'Well, I was shocked about Lomax. Our differences were only academic. Stimulating, really. You know.'

Patrick did.

'I'll miss him. And he's a loss to scholarship. He wasn't a depressive. Or if he was, it was a new thing. You can't tell, these days. Lucy Amberley may know about that aspect.'

'I'd better get up there,' Patrick said.

'If you don't find her, she lives in Berkshire — Hungerford, that's the place.'

'Ah — good. If I don't find her up on Parnassus,' said Patrick, 'I'll look for her in Berkshire.'

V

Lucy Amberley would have to descend by the Sacred Way and emerge through the main entrance of the sanctuary if she were to rejoin the party from the *Persephone* at their coaches. She would be describing the same route as Vera Hastings, some distance behind. Patrick paid yet another entrance fee and walked fairly rapidly up the first part of the ascent. It would have taken Lucy some time to reach the stadium from the town and it was reasonable to assume she would rest there for a while; the rest of the party had been in the museum for about three-quarters of an hour.

From Marlow's description she sounded so ordinary that it might be easy to overlook her: smallish, fairish, forty-ish. Why had he never thought that Felix might have a mistress? Now he came to think about it, it was obvious. He and Gwenda had gone their separate ways years before; he must have needed someone; everyone did, though not everyone found what they needed. Patrick was glad that Felix had succeeded, and hoped that he would like the lady.

But perhaps she wasn't Felix's mistress. Marlow might have been mistaken.

He stopped frequently as he climbed and looked around for a smallish woman in a lavender dress. The colour caught his eye in the theatre, right up among the highest tiered seats. He climbed aloft to find the wearer was a Japanese. Patrick moved away. There were a number of Japanese sightseers climbing about among the rocks and the dried-up grasses and withered flowers. Most women seemed to be wearing brightly printed fabrics, or white dresses; Marlow had seemed a little vague about Lucy's dress, though not the colour of her eyes. He was not the sort of man to notice female attire in detail; it would have been wise to have asked one of the women in the group to confirm the description, but it was too late to think of that now.

Patrick came to the stadium. It was very quiet up here; above, the peaks of the Great Ones brooded over the valley. A few people were seated around the vast area of the arena, scene of so many past triumphs. In those days the air must have been full of shrill cries; here the original Charioteer had driven round in glory to the plaudits of the crowd.

Patrick walked along one side of the amphitheatre look-ing for a lavender dress. What would be the best approach when he found Lucy Amberley? Should he at once reveal the reason for his interest, or should he merely try to pick her up? It wasn't so outrageous; he would soon be forty-ish himself, he thought glumly.

He soon realized that in fact there were quite a lot of people in the stadium, some seated, some strolling around, some stationary, standing on the great blocks of stone taking photographs. It was only because the area was so vast that they seemed few. He saw several solitary ladies. One was a beefy girl in tight-packed jeans, bra-less under her clinging cotton sweater; she wore huge dark glasses and had tangled curls reaching half-way down her back. Another was elderly, seventy at a guess, with plimsolled feet and panama hat, the guide to Delphi in German in her hand. Various others were scattered about but most people were in pairs or groups. He had not seen Vera Hastings as he came up: by now she was probably reviving herself in the *taverna* below.

He turned to look back at the entrance and saw a distant, solitary figure leaving the arena. Against the light he could not distinguish the colour she wore, but some instinct told him that this was his quarry; he hastened in pursuit.

On the whole, except when the tourist coaches toot their horns impatiently to summon wayward passengers, people do not move at speed along the winding paths of Parnassus, so he soon caught up with her. Back view, he saw the straw hat, a plain bluey-mauve cotton dress, and rather good legs. He strolled along behind her. She was proceeding slowly, delving in her bag for something. Then she blew her nose, quite hard. It was unexpected in this setting; the dry heat had a dehydrating effect on all bodily functions. Either she had a summer cold, or she was weeping.

She began to move faster, blundering down the steep path; two people brushed against her, coming up: Elsie and George. Patrick had to stop to speak to them. George's dark, alert face wore an eager look; they had been in the sanctuary for hours. Here was a man who had expected wonders and found that they exceeded all his dreams; Patrick curbed his impatience while they talked. Then the Loukases went on and he continued his descent. By this time Lucy Amberley had disappeared; she might have wandered from the main path but at least he now knew whom he sought.

He soon saw her under a tree looking down towards the theatre. She was sitting on a stone and tears were pouring silently down her face. Patrick felt himself to be a gross intruder on her grief; he halted, ready to retreat, but he dislodged a stone on the path and she heard him. She started, turned her head away and began mopping operations with her handkerchief.

Patrick hesitated, but he had already disturbed her, so he plunged.

'Mrs Amberley — I'm sorry — but I knew Felix Lomax,' he said.

At first she did not respond. Then she turned and looked at him blankly.

'I met Giles Marlow just now. He said you were a friend of Felix's. So was I. My name is Grant. Patrick Grant. We were colleagues.'

She repeated his name.

'Oh yes. Felix spoke of you,' she said.

'Shall I go away?' He could not bear to see her distress.

'No — no. It's all right. I'm being idiotic,' she said.

He sat down at a little distance from her on the low wall and looked in a different direction, while she regained her self-control. Then he heard her voice.

'You see, I just don't understand it. It was such a cruel way to die.'

She sounded calmer, so Patrick turned to face her.

'I don't understand it either,' he said. 'I wondered why he went to Crete.'

'So do I,' she said.

'He didn't tell you?'

'No. He just left a note — he didn't even say goodbye. He hoped to rejoin us in a few days, when we got back from Turkey. At least by the time we came here, I'd expected.'

Patrick looked round at the towering mountains above them, the steep-sided valley below with the silvered olive trees and the greener pines. She had been here with Felix. An immense pity for her grief filled him.

'I've given myself away. The situation must be obvious to you, Dr Grant,' she said. 'Not that it matters now.'

'I'd no idea,' he said, inadequately.

She shrugged, and managed a smile.

'We'd been moderately discreet,' she said. 'But that was over. He'd decided to end that charade of a marriage. We'd hoped to get Gwenda to agree to a divorce. But anyway he could have got one eventually.'

'Did Gwenda know?'

'Yes. He told her before he came away.'

'How did she react?'

'With bitterness.' Lucy twisted a piece of dried-up grass between her fingers. She had shapely hands. 'An uncle of Felix's died in March and left him a lot of money.'

'I didn't know.'

'Why should you? It was rather a surprise to Felix.'

'Why didn't you do it before? Marry, I mean, or at least get together?'

'He wanted to wait till his daughter was settled. And I have two sons. They're more or less adult now. Odd as it may seem, we didn't want to set all the young ones a bad example.'

At least she wouldn't be totally bereft, if she had two sons. Patrick had tried not to stare at her, but he was curious. In a way she did look ordinary, as Marlow had implied, but her face was marred by her weeping. Her eyes were lovely, though; huge, and of a deep, unusual blue, just like her dress. There was a total lack of affectation about her that was enabling her to get through this unconventional meeting without embarrassment.

'How good that Felix met you,' said Patrick simply, and then, 'how did it happen?'

'On one of the cruises. Four years ago.'

It had been easy for them both, aboard the *Persephone*. The next year she had joined the cruise again. Then Felix had gone on two cruises a year, and so had she.

'It was idyllic, really, in this sort of setting. It couldn't last, I suppose,' she said.

They had spent more and more time together at home. Her cottage in Hungerford was easily reached from Oxford. Had Gwenda known about it before Felix told her?

Talking was doing Lucy good. She must have been putting up a brave front aboard the *Persephone*.

'What about some coffee, or a drink? You need something,' Patrick said. 'Shall we go to the *taverna* down the road?'

'But I'm taking up your time.'

'You're not. I'm delighted that we met.' Should he tell her why he was here? No — or anyway, not yet. 'I'm staying in Delphi. I've plenty of time,' he said.

'You're very kind.'

He wasn't. He was anxious to get her into a condition where she could stand more questions.

They walked on down the mountain-side together.

'No wonder Apollo chose this place,' said Patrick.

'It's dramatic, isn't it? It's easy to shut one's eyes and be carried backwards in time. That old oracle must have been rather a witch-like female.'

'Mm. Full of dope, do you think?' asked Patrick.

'Maybe. Anyway the priests interpreted her mutterings. They could have alleged she said anything.'

Some gardeners were at work on the Stoa of the Athenians, chipping away with trowels like those masons use, triangular and pointed. The black-clad women had scarves wound round their heads, wimple-like; they bent low, working slowly in the sunlight, dislodging flowering weeds from the crevices between the stones. One led a laden donkey away.

'They must have been using trowels like that here for centuries,' said Lucy.

'Yes.' Patrick looked at the women. How patiently they toiled; no modern weedkillers were used here.

'When do you have to be back at the ship?' he asked.

'Oh, not for ages. Four o'clock. There's another party at Ossios Loukas. I said I'd get a taxi back to Itea.'

They walked down the road and crossed over to the *taverna* on the corner. Below it, the path led first to the gymnasium and then on down to the Tholos. It was cool here, under the shaded roof. Lucy asked for a long, cold drink. She must be tired; she had walked a considerable distance since leaving the coach. Patrick ordered lemonade for both of them.

When their drinks had arrived, and after she had sipped some of hers, he said:

'I found Felix's body.'

She did not start or exclaim. She merely looked at him in silence. After a few seconds she said:

'The papers didn't mention that. Tell me about it.'

He regarded her gravely. She was quite composed now. The big blue eyes returned his gaze steadily. She had a right to know.

He told her, leaving out the distressing details of Felix's condition after several days submerged.

'I'm glad it was you, and not a stranger,' she said, when he had finished, and he began to wish he had done more: offered to cope with Felix's papers and seen his body safely on to the plane. 'Do you think it was an accident?' she added. 'The police did, I know.'

He parried this.

'Do you?'

'I don't know what to think. He hated heights.'

'Yes. But he came here — to Delphi—'

'He was all right in this sort of place, as long as he didn't look directly over a precipice. He didn't like standing high up above the theatre, for example, but he didn't have to.' She laughed, a little wryly. 'He was always the one who stayed below and declaimed something from the stage for everyone else to listen to, above.'

'You can't imagine him walking on a cliff top?'

'Not willingly.'

Patrick plunged.

'You don't think he committed suicide, do you?'

'No. Not for a minute,' she said at once. 'He would never do that.'

Now that he had met Lucy Amberley any lingering doubts Patrick might have had about that had gone. Felix had a lot to live for. And he hadn't had a heart attack; his death was caused by drowning.

'But — what else could explain it?' she said.

He did not answer.

'Someone — might have pushed him?' She could hardly utter it.

'I don't know. I don't see how they got him up on the top of the cliff in the first place. And who would want to do it?' Patrick said. 'But why did he go to Crete? If we knew that, we might be able to find out more.'

Lucy was shaken by the new idea but she made an effort to absorb it calmly.

'I asked, in the ship,' she said. 'You know — if he'd mentioned anything to anyone. We'd all flown out that morning. Then he'd taken a party on a quick tour round Venice. I went aboard and got settled in — I'd been on Felix's lightning tours before — a sprint round the Doge's Palace and St. Mark's, then the Bridge of Sighs.' She smiled at the memory. 'We intended to spend a week there after the cruise.'

'He must have had a message,' said Patrick. 'Someone must have cabled him.'

'They thought that, on board. But there was no trace of any cable. They'd have known, in the ship. Everyone thought he must have been sent for from home.'

Gwenda: had she wired him to meet her? But why in Crete? He'd inherited money and planned to leave her.

'Had he made a will recently?' Patrick demanded.

Lucy looked shocked.

'I haven't the slightest idea,' she said. Then she realized what he was thinking. 'Oh no,' she said. 'Never.'

Gwenda had been at home when given the news of Felix's death. That much Patrick knew from what Inspector Manolakis had told him. But he'd been dead for several days. Gwenda could have travelled out, killed him, and returned home in time to receive the news.

It was fantastic. How would she have contrived to lure him to Crete?

'The Greek police don't think he was — murdered, do they?' said Lucy.

Patrick thought of the clever, industrious Inspector.

'They seemed quite satisfied,' he said. He would have to go back to Crete. If necessary he must describe this conversation to Manolakis. There would be a way of tracing Gwenda's movements; her passport would be stamped if she had used it. There was Interpol and Scotland Yard.

He could get hold of Scotland Yard himself. Before stirring up the police in Crete again he would get Colin to find out what Gwenda had been doing lately.

Thinking of Colin reminded him of the other odd business, which had been driven from his mind by thoughts of Felix. By now Jeremy Vaughan and his party of students would have arrived at Gatwick, and the mystery of the island of Mikronisos might have been revealed.

VI

Patrick took Lucy back to the hotel for lunch. It was only a short walk from the *taverna* to where he had left the car; she was glad to get into it and he saw that she was wrung out with emotion.

Once more the hotel lounge seemed blissfully cool. Another coachload of Americans had just arrived; some Britons were there too, and a party of Swedes. To and fro plodded the porters. Patrick's muscles screamed in silent sympathy.

He took Lucy to his room so that she might use his bathroom, which he thought she would like better than the cloakroom; then he left her, saying he would meet her by the bar.

He was waiting there for her, having ordered beer for them both, when Vera Hastings appeared; she came and sat beside him.

'I've had a lovely morning,' she told him. 'Those friends of yours, the Loukases, brought me back in a taxi. Wasn't that kind?'

'I'm so glad. Let me get you a drink,' Patrick suggested. 'What shall it be?'

She pondered a bit, then chose ouzo, which she said she was learning to like. Their drinks had just arrived when Lucy Amberley came up to them. She looked refreshed; the traces

of her tears had all been washed away. Patrick began to introduce them, but both were smiling in a surprised but pleased
manner.

'We know each other,' Lucy said.

It turned out that Lucy taught French part-time at a school
near her home; she was a customer of the bank where Vera
Hastings worked and they had been meeting over the counter
several times a month for years. They all lunched together; there
was really no option, and perhaps it was as well to form a trio
and keep the emotional temperature down. After her ouzo Vera
ceased to be shy, and enthused about Greece; she was bound
for Mycenae on Wednesday but planned to rest the day before.

'You can't do excursions every day,' she said. 'I must see
all I can — I'll never have another chance to come to Greece.'

While they were lunching the Loukases joined them.
They had decided to go back to Athens that afternoon on the
coach; Vera would be on it too. Patrick did not offer to drive
them; he meant to take Lucy back to Itea to rejoin the ship
and he did not want to be tied to a definite schedule. It might
be, when they talked again after the others had gone, that she
would decide to leave the cruise and press for more enquiries
into the manner of Felix's death.

They discussed their holiday experiences during lunch.
Lucy had collected herself again; she made an effort to be
bright; only now and then Patrick saw her attention slide away
and a blank expression come into her eyes. Continuing the
cruise must be very painful for her.

The other three hurried away after lunch to pack up their
things and find the coach; Vera was nervous in case it went
without them, and was clearly glad to cling to the Loukases.

'It's odd how you keep running into people on this sort of
holiday. I met the Loukases in Crete originally,' said Patrick.

They hadn't referred to Crete for almost two hours.

'Had you thought of leaving the ship? Going home, perhaps?' he asked Lucy.

She nodded.

'But what could I say? How could I explain? It's better to see it out. After all, there's plenty to do, and people are being kind — the few who knew, like Giles Marlow. The ordinary passengers know nothing about it, so they behave quite naturally to me. They may think I'm slightly demented, I seem to be so forgetful, but that's about all. By the time we get back I'll have had a chance to get used to it.'

'I wish there were some way to help,' said Patrick. He wondered about her; was she a widow, or divorced? He could see why Felix had been drawn to her for she was the antithesis of Gwenda: fair, where Gwenda was dark; gentle, where Gwenda was bossy; tender, he was certain.

She saw him looking at her with concern, and smiled.

'I'll be all right. I'll manage,' she said. 'It's just going to take some adjustment.'

She would go back to her life as it had been before Felix: the school; her house; and spasmodic, doubtless diminishing contact with her adult sons. There were widows all over the place; people were often alone. But if you found this rare thing, this other person who made you come alive, and then lost him — how dreadful.

'I don't suppose I'll come back to Greece,' Lucy was saying.

'You're content about Felix? To know no more, I mean?'

'No, not really. But I don't see what can be done. It's over — finished — nothing can bring him back.'

'But if Gwenda—' he did not finish. It could not be the answer.

'There's the daughter to be thought of,' Lucy said. 'You can't be right about Gwenda, it's too horrible to contemplate. But suppose you were, what would that girl think? She's a nice child, I've met her several times. And her husband's a good young man, quiet but determined. They're emigrating. Gwenda won't leave them alone so they feel it's the only way. They're not telling her until just before they go. So it may be better not to probe.'

She seemed to accept it. Perhaps she was right. But she had not seen Felix sodden, bloated, undignified in death.

'I'm glad we met,' she said. 'You've helped me.'

He took her down to Itea to rejoin the ship. He had accomplished very little, but he too was glad they had met.

He stopped for a swim before going back to Athens. On the way he passed numerous coaches; he was not sure which one carried the Loukases and Vera Hastings. He was glad to be alone; he had had enough of people for the day.

By the time he reached the outskirts of Athens he had decided to ask Colin Smithers to discover the terms of Felix's will and to make discreet enquiries about Gwenda's movements the week before. It would do no harm. Once that idea was disposed of, one way or the other, he would make up his mind whether to talk to Manolakis.

He took the car back to the garage from which he had hired it, settled his expenses, and then went back to his hotel. The English papers had arrived and he bought one. A tiny paragraph on an inside page announced that police had arrested a man on a plane arriving from Athens at Gatwick on Sunday evening. No details were given.

He wondered, somewhat uneasily, if he was still a target for a contrived accident. He had felt free from threat in Delphi; the idea of personal menace was not pleasant.

VII

The reception clerk at the hotel looked anxious when Patrick asked for his key. The police had been enquiring after him; he was to telephone them as soon as he returned. He gave Patrick a slip of paper with the number he was required to ring. There was a cable, also. The man was too worried even to ask if he had enjoyed Delphi: this did not look the type of visitor to get mixed up in any trouble, but the clerk had seen enough of life to be surprised at nothing. Patrick said he would telephone from his room, and walked away, apparently unconcerned; but the clerk watched gravely until he had vanished into the lift.

The cable was from Colin Smithers and said, tersely: GRAVEN IMAGES NOT WEEDS.

So Arthur Winterton was not carrying drugs: that was a useful piece of information to have before he rang the Greek police. Scotland Yard must have had to communicate with their Greek counterparts no matter what the smuggled cargo, for they would have to get to the bottom of the trouble. He remembered that Elsie Loukas had said her husband was an archaeologist; he had been interested in Mikronisos before the war, and apparently it had been subjected to a volcanic eruption many centuries ago. Someone must have come upon some antique remains and be doing a corner in them. He recalled how the woman had suddenly appeared from below him that day, and the reflected light that he thought came from the glasses of someone watching.

Murcott might have gone further and found what lay below the sheer drop, and Murcott had died. It would have been easy to take his body back to the top on a donkey and toss it down to the spot where it was found. Someone had tried to push Patrick in front of a bus. But did people who stole art treasures dabble in murder? Were they so ruthless?

Was Felix's death linked in some way with Murcott's? If so, why Crete? But the *Psyche* had been in Crete and then at Mikronisos.

He was tired, and he wanted a shower and a drink. It was tempting to postpone telephoning the police until the next day; he had not definitely planned to return to Athens that night so they might never know when, in fact, he did get back. But they might ring again, and ask the clerk. And the matter was urgent. A man had died: two men, if there was a connection between their deaths; and someone had tried to harm Patrick himself. He telephoned.

Twenty minutes later a large black police car swept up to the hotel to collect him. He had snatched a quick shower in the interval, and his hair was still wet, slicked back for once from his forehead, as he hurried downstairs in response to the desk clerk's agitated summons.

The driver of the car spoke very little English so conversation on the way to headquarters was limited, but the officer into whose presence Patrick was taken was clearly very senior and he spoke good English. With him was a younger man whose English was fluent. They greeted him courteously, offered him a cigarette and a chair, and asked why he had got in touch with Scotland Yard.

'We thank you for it, Dr Grant. You must know that,' said the senior officer earnestly. 'But we want to know how you found out about the contraband.'

'What was he carrying? I thought it might be drugs,' said Patrick. 'Archaeological finds of some sort?'

'Votive offerings. Small figures, grave ornaments and jewellery. All very small, but worth very much money,' said the officer. 'Very, very old. You have to help us, please, Dr Grant. How did you know about this?'

Patrick thought the Greek officer showed great restraint in not giving him hell for tipping off the British police instead of the Athens force. He described what he had seen from his hotel window and how he had then met Arthur Winterton.

'I was in darkness in my room. They were not. When Winterton took the bag,' he said, 'they didn't see me.'

'They were careless, for professionals,' said the younger policeman.

'Perhaps they were not so professional in this matter,' said the older man.

'I think their plans must have miscarried,' said Patrick. This needed some help from the fluent young man before the older officer was clear about the meaning. Patrick explained that the incident in the hotel might have had a perfectly innocent explanation; it was only when he went to Mikronisos himself and felt he was being watched that he became really suspicious. He recounted the whole story.

'There was, some days before, that unfortunate accident on the island,' frowned the senior officer.

'Yes,' said Patrick. He added, 'The man who took the parcel — Arthur Winterton — is deaf. Now I realize that he is an expert lip-reader. He sat facing me at dinner, but some way further down the table, when I told Miss Watson I was going to the island the next day. He could have interpreted our conversation.'

'Hm. So you think he warned his associates to watch for you?'

'Yes.' Or he could have come himself, aboard the *Psyche*, after the funeral. He said he was going to the Benaki museum; no one would have doubted him. The *Psyche* had been at

Mikronisos at twelve: no, it could not be done in the time. If Arthur Winterton had gone to the island he had taken some other boat to get there. So he need not mention the *Psyche* even though there was some connection between Spiro's friend, the young man with the moustache, and the man who had given Arthur Winterton the parcel, for he had seen them together on the Acropolis. Patrick was hoping very much that the *Psyche* was not mixed up in this affair; he did not want to find that Jill McLeod was involved with thieves, and even murderers.

'This will not be the first time that precious remains have left the country in this way,' said the senior police officer. 'But we must stop it. We will see what there is on Mikronisos.' He said something in Greek to the other man, who nodded. 'Before the war some German archaeologists were planning to dig on that island. But the war came and it was never done. No one has tried since, but we believe the British have expressed interest.'

'So someone who knew about that might have had a go alone,' said Patrick slowly.

'Yes. Or something might have been found by accident. There are plans for building a hotel. While surveying, some traces may have been found. We will discover the truth, Dr Grant. There is much to do.'

Patrick could see that there was. They let him go at last, when he had given as full a description as he could of the man whom Arthur Winterton had visited. He promised not leave Athens without telling the police, and he was escorted back to the hotel by the younger officer, who inspected his room, identified the one opposite where the transaction had taken place, bade Patrick a brisk goodnight and then went into a huddle with the management about the identity of recent guests.

By this time Patrick was extremely hungry. He was about to go in search of dinner when the telephone rang. It was his sister Jane, calling from England.

'Thank goodness I've found you. Are you all right?' she exclaimed.

'Perfectly, thanks. Why shouldn't I be?'

'Wherever you go, you keep getting mixed up in things,' she said. 'Colin rang me from Scotland Yard.'

'Well, this isn't my show — it's up to the police,' said Patrick. 'They're very busy this end.'

'So they are here. That man, Arthur Winterton, is dead.'

'What?'

'Yes. He was let out on bail. He fell in front of an underground train. It was on the news tonight. And Colin confirmed it.'

'But he must have already spilt the beans,' said Patrick. 'Or not?'

'Not wholly, I gather, but a good few.'

'Oh dear,' said Patrick. 'This does sound rather nasty.'

'Come home. Or go to Corfu.'

'I won't do that. I've things to attend to,' said Patrick grandly. 'I may go back to Crete. I'm not happy about the Lomax business. Did Colin mention it?'

'He did.' She sighed. 'You won't learn, will you?'

When they had both hung up he thought, tetchily, how she fussed. But then, it would be sad if there were no one who minded what became of him. Still, he did not want her to worry. He couldn't believe that he was now in any danger himself; he'd already seen the police, and if the villains were watching him they would know that. If they had heard of Winterton's arrest they would be clearing out of Mikronisos as fast as they could. He would not have been their only courier; other respectable-seeming tourists were probably taking fertility idols and oil jars back in their reticules each week. Stealing archaeological remains and disposing of them illegally was a deplorable business, but killing people who found out what was happening or got caught was a great deal worse. For of course Arthur Winterton must have been murdered too.

Patrick's brain was churning with all this, and his stomach was churning from want of food.

He would go to the Plaka for dinner, where there would be music.

Even so, he picked up *Martin Chuzzlewit*, for company.

He had neglected to give the police the squashed cigarette stub he had preserved so carefully.

VIII

Patrick went to the *taverna* where he had lunched on the day of his arrival in Athens; then, it had been quiet, but now it was busy. Most of the tables were occupied, and three bouzouki musicians were playing. The music throbbed, hauntingly plaintive yet stirring. Patrick had almost finished his meal when he saw Jill McLeod walk past the low wall surrounding the garden where he sat. She was alone, and although she glanced in at the diners, she did not see him in his corner under the mulberry tree.

He was up and after her in a flash, and when she recognized him the dejected expression on her face fled. He invited her to join him, but she said she had already eaten. However, she thought she could manage some fruit salad, and she would help him to finish his wine. She returned with him to his table. She was dressed in the long, purple skirt he had seen her wearing before, and a skimpy black top.

After she had drunk some wine, he said:

'Have you left the *Psyche?*'

She nodded.

'They put me ashore on Hydra. Made me take the ferry to Piraeus. Said they didn't want me any longer. After all these weeks.'

Thank goodness for that, thought Patrick.

'They?' he asked.

'Spiro and Yannis.'

'Yannis?' Patrick almost shot off his chair at the name.

'Spiro's friend. Oh, you never met him.'

'The short man with the moustache? Older than Spiro?' As if he did not know it! Of course, it had been staring him in the face the whole time: and the mother: the woman on Mikronisos was Ilena. It must be so.

'Mm,' said Jill. 'I didn't like him much. There was always trouble when he was around.'

'What was his other name?' asked Patrick, just to be sure. 'His surname?'

But Jill had never heard it.

'Have some more wine,' said Patrick, and ordered another bottle.

In the end she told him all she knew, for she was hurt and unhappy, and glad to have found a friend and sympathy.

Yannis had appeared during June. Each time he came, Spiro had to make special trips away from Crete. He had been to Mikronisos several times, and to a rendez-vous with another boat off the coast of Libya. That time, various boxes had been loaded aboard, and both Spiro and Yannis had been very nervous. They had gone on to Mikronisos afterwards. Jill hated those excursions for the sea often blew up and was very rough, and she had been seasick.

'What did you do on the island?' asked Patrick.

Sometimes they took passengers. They unloaded the boxes there, too. The passengers varied but there was often a man she heard called Kamal. She described him, and the description fitted the man who had given Arthur Winterton the parcel.

'There was an Englishman, too,' she said. 'Last Saturday. Very deaf, with a hearing aid.' They'd collected him at sea; he'd been brought out to their meeting place by a speedboat from somewhere, one of those vessels that carved through the sea at incredible speed. They'd dropped him back at Piraeus

159

in the evening. The *Psyche* had a good engine and could make fair speed herself in calm seas.

'Yannis's mother lives on Mikronisos. We picked her up on Saturday too, from the harbour, and took her round to Kamal's house on the other side,' said Jill.

'Yannis's mother?' Patrick was cautious.

'Yes. She housekeeps or something for Kamal. Ilena, she's called. She's nice. Doesn't speak much English. I think she's a bit scared of Yannis,' said Jill. 'Imagine being scared of your own son!'

It was not an uncommon condition, in Patrick's experience. But he had learned enough.

'What are your plans now?' he asked her.

'Oh, I don't know. Maybe I'll go on to Turkey,' she said vaguely.

'Aren't you due to go back to college?'

'I'm due to begin. But I can put it off for a year,' she said. 'I might go to England. My folks aren't expecting me home yet.' She sounded slightly wistful and Patrick seized on this.

'Go home,' he said. 'Go back to Canada and get stuck in to your studies. You've had a splendid experience over here, but work's the best cure now.'

'I don't need a cure,' Jill said stubbornly. She drew a picture on the tablecloth with a knife. 'Spiro had another girl all the time.'

'Sophia,' said Patrick.

Jill stared at him.

'How did you know?'

'I'm psychic,' said Patrick. He thought for a minute. 'No more passengers aboard the *Psyche?*' he asked.

There had been others besides Kamal, men who ignored her and jabbered away in Greek too fast for her to follow, she said. 'And there was the English professor. We met him in Heraklion and took him to Challika with us. We often stopped off in Heraklion for stores,' she added.

'An English professor? When was that?'

'About ten days ago — no, more.' She racked her brains.
'A nice old boy. He drank ouzo all the way.'

'Did you meet him by appointment?'

'No. Spiro ran into him in some bar and they got talking. He was looking for someone, he said, but they weren't in Heraklion so he was going to try Challika.'

'Did he tell you his name?'

'No.'

'How did you know he was a professor, then?'

'He just looked like one. And he spoke funny Greek — old-fashioned, Spiro said.'

'What did he look like?' demanded Patrick.

'Oh — oldish. Thin hair, you know, and a bit wrinkly. He limped, too.'

It must have been Felix. Though he would not have been pleased to hear himself described as oldish; he was fifty-four. It accounted for the ouzo, too, which Felix had drunk before death.

'Where did you put him ashore? At the harbour?'

'No, we didn't. He asked us to put him off just below that old war-time fort or whatever it is. You know.'

'The pillbox?'

'Is that what they're called? How funny.'

'What an odd arrangement. Why did he want to go ashore there?'

'He said he'd be staying at one of the hotels near there and it would save a walk.'

'Did he have any luggage?'

'Just one small bag.'

That fitted. Lucy said he had left most of his stuff aboard the *Persephone*.

'What time of day did you put him ashore?'

'Oh, in the evening. It was nearly dark. He stumbled off over the rocks.'

'Carrying his suitcase? He didn't forget it?'

'It wasn't a suitcase. More like a holdall, you know, with a zip across. He took it.'

Where was that, then?

'Did you see him again?'

'No. Never. I wondered about that. You keep seeing people, in a small place like that.'

She might never have heard of the drowning. The police were very discreet. But she had been one of the last people to see Felix alive.

'Please go home to Canada, Jill,' Patrick said. 'Tomorrow, if possible. Have you your fare?'

IX

He took her back to his hotel and found, greatly to his relief, that they had a room free for her. She had left her luggage at the station, so they fetched that in a taxi and then went upstairs.

Jill was disappointed at being banished to a room of her own and came to his to say so. He had plied her generously with wine to make her talk freely, and now had to face the consequences. At least she did not bracket him with Felix as being oldish, he thought, with wry relief, untwining her arms from around his neck. He felt vulnerable, but wanted no complications. He did not favour one-night stands with rejected young damsels.

Outside, Athens still throbbed with life. They would go out, he decided, and told her so.

'Have you ever been up Mount Lykabettos?' he demanded. She had not.

'Right. Then that's where we'll go. Get a sweater or something, it may be windy up there. I'll meet you downstairs in five minutes. Now scoot.'

She made a face at him, but she smiled and left. He reflected that not twenty-four hours ago he had been fantasizing about luscious young blondes; now here was one, and he was treating her as if she were ten years old.

While she was getting her sweater he went downstairs himself and set the desk-clerk to finding out about planes to Montreal. If one left the next morning and had a spare seat he was to book the girl on to it. Patrick had discovered that she had kept her fare home intact, a promise she had made to her parents; had this not been so he would have paid it himself, to have made sure of her safety.

'We're walking,' he said, when she arrived in the foyer carrying a much-washed Arran-knit cardigan over her arm. 'It's not very far.'

If he got her physically tired she would be less trouble when they returned, assuming she continued to feel affectionately drawn to him.

She slid her hand into the crook of his arm as they set off down the road; it felt curiously comforting, and he let it remain. Her flowing skirt flapped round her legs and caught against his as they walked through Constitution Square, past the Parliament Building and on towards Kolonaki.

'This is the expensive part of Athens. The smart area,' he told her severely, striding along so that she was almost running to keep up. Her travels had not taken her to many such places, he was sure. He took her along Ploutarchou and showed her the British Embassy; her own consulate must be somewhere around here too, he supposed. At least he was saving them trouble, by getting her out. For she had agreed to go home.

He was worrying in case they were being followed. Reason told him that Kamal and his friends would be too busy saving their own necks to be after his; but they had got rid of Arthur Winterton. They must have agents well dispersed over the globe. At least, in the hotel, he and Jill would have been safe from that sort of attack; it would be dreadful if, by bringing her out, he had exposed her to danger. But the gang would hesitate to involve Jill again, surely? She had been ditched; if she were assaulted now the trail would lead directly back to the culprits themselves, for someone would remember having seen her aboard the *Psyche*.

He felt happier when his reflections reached this point and gave her hand an encouraging pat. As they approached the foot of the shining, cone-like mountain there were fewer people about; he was sure that no one was following them. All the same, how could one tell for certain? He took great care at every street crossing.

Jill cheered up when they reached the funicular station at the bottom of Lykabettos and boarded the train. There were a number of other passengers in their cabin, but this did not prevent her from clinging to him fondly; she said the funicular reminded her of ski-trips back home. She had not mentioned Spiro for some time; once away from Greece she would soon recover. Her pride had been hurt, as well as her heart, by the manner of her dismissal. Patrick had told her nothing about the activities of her former friends; the less she knew the better.

She exclaimed with genuine delight about the view from the top of the mountain, and went silent in the church, which smelled of incense and glittered with gold and silver adornments. Then she yawned. So she was tiring; that was something. He'd walk her all the way back; that should do the trick. They moved towards the stairs at the side of the church and started the descent; as they did so two people who had been leaning on the parapet looking across the city turned also, to go the other way to the funicular. The woman's white hair caught Patrick's attention and he recognized Ursula Norris. She was holding the arm of a man about her own age, slightly shorter than she was; he had strongly marked brows, a fine, jutting nose, and thick iron-grey hair. Patrick knew at once by his clothes and his whole aspect that he was Greek. They were totally absorbed in one another and she did not notice Patrick standing only a few feet away.

He was guilty of staring rudely for an instant in surprise. So this was why she had been eager to reach Athens; this explained the faint air of excitement she had about her; this was why she had no definite return date fixed.

Jill tugged at his sleeve.

'Come on, if we're going,' she said. 'But I wish we could ride down in the funi.'

They certainly could not, now. Patrick would never willingly embarrass Ursula, although there was nothing in the least furtive about her manner with her companion. After all, why should there be?

'We're walking,' he said firmly.

They set off through the darkness, Jill clinging tightly to Patrick's arm. The path wound spirally round the mountain, and at the base Patrick turned the wrong way. They went down some wide steps into an unfamiliar street, and he realized that they were too far north. In the end they took a taxi back to the centre of the city. Jill curled up against him in the cab and laid her mane of curly fair hair on his shoulder. It smelt of the sea. He let it remain, and took her hand, patting it paternally.

'You must get yourself into lots of trouble, Jill, behaving like this with strange men,' he said.

'You're not strange. I've known you a week,' she said, drawing closer. He resisted the urge to put an arm around her, and detached her when the taxi stopped. The driver looked at him with some admiration as he paid. Am I so advanced in age that it is a matter for marvelling if a young girl seems to like me, he wondered indignantly, paying.

They collected their keys. The clerk had secured a booking on a plane that left for Montreal at ten minutes to ten in the morning, with a change at Frankfurt. Patrick made Jill draft out a cable to her parents telling them to expect her, and the clerk promised to send it. That way, if she did not arrive, someone would start wondering where she was. Then they went upstairs.

Patrick took Jill to her door, opened it, and made sure that all was well inside.

'Now get to bed, Jilly,' he said. He knew her name, but she had never asked his; funny girl.

'That's what my Dad calls me, Jilly,' she said.

It had slipped out; how odd.

'I'll see you get up in time for the plane,' he said.

Before he could escape she latched on to him and twined her arms round his neck, with her warm mouth on his. She was young and soft, and very unhappy; she needed consoling. Patrick's reflexes started to function but he unwound her firmly. Some nice young Canadian lad could do the consoling in twenty-four hours.

'Lock yourself in,' he commanded, and let himself out. He stood outside her room, recovering, and mopping his face with his handkerchief. After a few minutes he heard the key turn and then the bed creak. She would sleep till he woke her.

He went back down to the hall to check on the plane. The ticket could be collected on the way to the airport and the cable had gone. The clerk had been very efficient and Patrick tipped him generously. Then he went up to bed.

What a day it had been.

Martin Chuzzlewit was no companion tonight. It was a long time before he slept.

PART FIVE:
TUESDAY AND WEDNESDAY

ATHENS

I

Though muted because his room was at the back of the building, the increased traffic noise of early morning woke Patrick soon after six. He could hear a bulldozer nearby. Wherever one walked in the city concrete blocks were being raised or demolished, workmen toiled under bamboo shades, and the air was full of white dust and the din of machinery. It added to the general feeling of vitality that abounded; that was it: that was the mainspring of the Greek enchantment: the people's zest for life. Despite all the disasters that had struck their country throughout its long history their spirit survived triumphant. Cheered by this philosophical conclusion, Patrick fell briefly asleep again, but a sound like a house falling down roused him once more; it probably was a house falling down. He telephoned for breakfast to be brought to his room, ordered Jill's to be sent to hers, too, and then rang her up. It was time she woke.

It occurred to him that he should have sunk his scruples the night before; who would have lost, if he had? At least he would have made sure that she did not change her mind and do a moonlight flit.

But she hadn't. Her voice answered, sounding sleepy.

He told her breakfast was on its way and she must get up.

'Oh—' Yawn. 'Can't I have it with you?' But it was said half-heartedly.

'I've finished mine,' he lied. 'Besides, you'll need a bath, won't you, before the journey?' It was a hint. Her bare feet in their thonged sandals had been distinctly dusty the night before, though he hadn't found their grubbiness the least repellent. The impression she gave was one of wholesomeness; he would like to think that this was why he had not succumbed.

'What time must I be ready?' she asked, like a child.

He told her, and said he would collect her from her room.

She was waiting when he knocked on her door. Her hair was tied into a pony-tail and she looked below the age of consent, attired in faded but clean jeans, a clean cotton sweater and holding an anorak.

'Well, breakfast all right?' he asked heartily. My God, I sound like a hospital nurse, he thought.

'Mm, fine, I was glad of the egg,' she said. He had ordered her one. Unlike the hotel in Crete, this one provided crisp breakfast rolls, but a couple of them were not enough foundation for a long journey. It might be some time before she was fed on the plane.

'Right, then.' He picked up her case. 'We'll collect your ticket on the way to the airport.'

She had her fare money in travellers' cheques. Patrick thought she had done well to keep them intact, and also not to have lost them during her adventures. But doubtless Spiro had supplied her with food as well as a share of his berth in the boat. All went without a hitch; the ticket was waiting and they reached the airport with time to spare.

'It's nice of you to see me off,' she said.

'It's not much fun, travelling alone,' he answered.

'Oh, I don't know. Things kind of happen,' she said.

Patrick hoped she would not get deflected from Montreal by anything that happened on the way. They filled in the time before her flight was called by having more coffee. He was not going to leave until he was certain that, short of fleeing when on the runway, she had gone. He hoped her nerve would last during the stop at Frankfurt. Once she saw the Air Canada plane there, with its red maple leaf emblem, the thought of home might keep her going. He asked her about her family, and soon she was telling him, happily enough, about her two younger brothers, her doctor father, and their summer lakeside hut. The rather forlorn look she had worn on the ride to the airport disappeared while she talked.

Jill was sitting strapped into her seat in the Lufthansa jet before she realized that she did not know the Englishman's name.

Patrick felt oddly bereft when the plane was safely airborne. Although he was relieved to see the last of her, she had certainly been an invigorating companion. He cleaned his glasses and wondered what to do next. The urgency of getting Jill away from further involvement in whatever her former companions had been doing had driven deeper thoughts about their activities out of his mind. Alec Mudie would not have been pleased to know that his godson had been busy smuggling antiquities out of Greece. Why had Yannis involved his mother in his malpractice? It was easy to see why he had misled Alec about his reasons for not leaving Greece; he would know which sort of offence Alec would prefer him to commit. The attitude of the men of Ai Saranda was explained, too; they may not have known just what Yannis was doing, but they clearly suspected something not far from the truth.

He decided not to go back into Athens at once. He would go in the other direction, towards Sounion; he was on the way there already and a bus would soon take him further. He would get off when he saw a spot that looked pleasant and not too crowded, where he could walk and think.

An hour later he was sitting on a rock overlooking the sea while a gentle breeze blew. The sun beat down, but his head was protected by his Cretan straw hat. By this time Jill's plane would be somewhere over Italy. She would soon forget, or, if she did not do that, recall, after the hurt had gone, the good part of her Greek experience. If Yannis and Spiro were caught, as they probably would be, she would have had a great deal to regret; now she need never know about their shady activities. His own part in the business was over; he saw no need to tell the police about the *Psyche*, though they might find it out on their own; others had seen her off the island.

But had Felix known about the discoveries on Mikronisos? Had he met someone else carrying illicit treasures? If so, why Crete? And why not cancel his trip in the *Persephone* from England? Why wait till he got to Venice?

Felix had changed his plans because of something that had happened after leaving England. Since he had flown out with Lucy, and only left her a short note in the ship, the vital event must have taken place in Venice. He had toured quickly round with his pilgrims, visiting the most obvious places.

They had doubtless had drinks in the Piazza San Marco after visiting the Basilica. Everyone did.

What happened when you had drinks there?

Pigeons abounded, music played, and you met either your next-door neighbour or someone you had not seen for twenty years.

He was looking for someone, Jill had said. So he had met someone in Venice whom he wanted to see again. In the note to Lucy he had not mentioned Crete, so at the time of writing it, he could not have known his ultimate destination. Was he following someone? Why had he chosen to go to Challika aboard the *Psyche* and not by bus or by taxi? Had he wanted to keep his arrival secret? He had strangely elected to climb ashore over the rocks, rather than land reasonably at the jetty. It looked as if he wanted to arrive unobserved.

It was too hot, sitting here in the sun, in spite of his hat. Patrick got up and strolled on.

Ursula Norris was staying near here. Why not ring her up and see if she would be free for lunch? She could always refuse, if she were too busy with her Greek friend. He could discuss the puzzle of Felix with her and see if she thought his death could be connected with the events on the island, about which she knew nothing. She would be interested to hear of them, he was sure, and anyway it would be pleasant to see her again.

Perhaps that had subconsciously been his intention when he decided to come out in this direction.

You wonder too much about why things happen, he told himself crossly.

Would he be able to manage the Greek public telephone system?

II

He was; it proved simple indeed, and Ursula answered at once. She was delighted to hear him and invited him round.

Perhaps he had hoped for that too, thought Patrick, in the mood to question every motive.

He accepted, was told how to find the villa, and soon arrived.

There were oleander trees in the garden, the blossoms fresh but the leaves dusty now that summer had lasted so long. A wide flight of shallow steps led up to the front door; geraniums bloomed in narrow beds close to the house. Ursula saw him coming up the path and opened the door before he could ring; she greeted him with obvious pleasure. He peered about furtively for signs of her companion of the night before, but she seemed to be alone.

'The maid's just gone,' she said, apparently reading his thoughts. 'Such luxury — she comes for three hours every morning. Come along.'

She led the way across a tiled hall into a small sitting-room. The floor was marble, with three rugs scattered on it; one set of windows, shuttered, overlooked the front of the house where the sun shone; another set, including a french door, led out on to a terrace shaded by a vine. Here there were several comfortable garden chairs and a table made of wrought-iron. A copy of *Clea* lay on the table. Ursula saw him look at it.

'Are you enjoying it?' he asked.

'A *tour de force*, but unpalatable,' she said promptly. 'I felt it had to be done. I'm going back to *Persuasion* next. It will be such a relief.'

Patrick laughed at this.

'Though lives do get muddled, and do intertwine most strangely,' Ursula allowed.

'Indeed they do,' said Patrick.

'Let me give you a drink. Then you can tell me what you've been doing in Athens,' she said.

'A bit of intertwining, you could say,' he said.

He told her about Delphi and the tourists worn out by the extent of their sight-seeing, and how he had met Vera Hastings again. She listened with interest. She had changed in the few days since they had last met; somehow, she was sparkling. Patrick felt cheered at the thought that the man he had seen her with was responsible for the alteration in her; was one never too old for love? Perhaps he need not, after all, settle for academic distinction and emotional famine.

'Ah — you look brighter. You walked up the path as if you were Atlas under his load,' said she. 'What's wrong?'

'It's a long story,' said Patrick.

'Never mind. Begin. Then we'll have lunch — just salad and cheese, and quite nice bread which Xanthe — that's the maid — brings. And fruit.'

'Xanthe. That's charming. Is she nymph-like? It sounds like the name of a nymph.

'It means blonde. She's not a nymph, she's fifty and stout,' said Ursula. 'And she's not blonde, either.'

'I thought Greeks were all named after saints?'

'They are, mostly. There aren't as many female saints as men.'

Patrick laughed again; he had found Ursula a good companion in Crete; now he felt she was a perfect one, witty and stimulating.

'I don't know what my parents had in mind when I was christened,' she went on. 'I can tell you that my life has not followed that of the saint whose name I bear.'

'Thank goodness,' said Patrick. 'Don't get transfixed by an arrow, please.'

'Too late,' she said. 'The damage is done,' and once more Patrick started laughing.

'I feel as if we've been friends for years,' he said.

'So do I, or I wouldn't talk like this,' said Ursula. 'It's the climate — and Greece. Now — tell me what's upsetting you.'

He told her all that had happened since he arrived in Athens. It took some time, and she made him stop in the middle while she brought their lunch out into the garden. He skated over his lecherous feelings for Jill but knew he did not deceive her.

'Do you make a habit of this?' she asked, when he had done.

'Of what? Despatching reckless young students back home?'

'No. Attracting dead bodies. Your average seems to be high.'

'It's happened before,' he admitted. 'That's why I don't treat it lightly.'

'You did well to get that girl out. She was obviously totally innocent. Useful camouflage, perhaps, for whatever they were doing.'

'The unfortunate man Murcott must have been innocent too.'

'You must be right about that. He must have stumbled on an illicit dig on that island.'

'Well, the police will know by now.'

'There's probably a tomb there.'

'Yes. I suppose they're dotted about all over the place waiting to be found.'

'Oh, certainly,' said Ursula. 'Are you sure the Yannis of the *Psyche* and the island is the one you were looking for?'

'He must be. Two Yannises with mothers called Ilena on one island — not possible, surely.'

'It does sound as if it would be stretching coincidence rather far,' she agreed. 'What are you going to do now?'

'Leave it, for the present. The police are busy enough with it all. I'm still worried about Felix. I may go back to Crete to see if I can find out more, now that I know he was aboard the *Psyche*.'

'Where will you begin?'

'I don't know. I could talk to Manolakis — the policeman.' He had not told her about Lucy Amberley, but now he did.

'Oh, poor woman,' said Ursula.

'It's awful, isn't it? What appalling things happen.'

'Yes. But they had some good moments together, from what you say. Some people miss out altogether,' said Ursula.

'You don't think the loss of something so — so precious, I suppose I mean,' said Patrick, rather embarrassed at having to use such a word in this context, 'is too much to be borne?'

'No, I don't.' Ursula was emphatic. 'It's not better to settle for no risks, if you have a choice.'

'There's always a moment like that, isn't there, when you decide to draw back, or go on?' said Patrick.

'Some people never recognize that moment of decision,' said Ursula seriously.

What had happened with her and her Greek? She had not chosen retreat; that was clear. Patrick longed to know the story. She was looking at him quizzically and he wondered what she was thinking. In fact, she had decided that he had just recovered from some blow to the heart and was afraid of further wounds.

'Tell me about Lucy,' she said.

He did, and that she knew Vera Hastings. This led on to how Vera had been in the Wrens during the war.

'You'd never think it,' marvelled Patrick. 'Those little round hats. And Elsie Loukas was one too, but they never met, it seems.'

'How did Elsie get to America? As a G.I. bride?'

'I don't think so, unless she had a husband between the one that was killed in Crete and George,' said Patrick. 'She's had her troubles. Deserted from the Wrens after some sort of nervous breakdown, and lived in dread of a court-martial. But as she had a baby, she'd have got out on that account, wouldn't she? It died though. I'm not sure of the sequence of events in her history.'

'Hm — how funny of her not to know.'

'Know what?'

'The Wrens weren't under military discipline. They could desert with impunity. But very few did. The army and air force took it more seriously.'

'Are you sure?'

'Yes. I was a Wren too,' said Ursula. 'But I wore a three-cornered hat.'

III

Athens was grilling when Patrick got back to the city. He went into the Zappeion Gardens behind the Parliament Building and sat on a seat in the shade to think. At first his mind raced round in circles but after a while his thoughts steadied and began to take definite shape. Little incidents came back to him, each insignificant in itself but adding up to one thing. He got up at last and walked back to the central post office on Eolou to send some cables. Then he went to the Archaeological Museum where he looked at the objects from Mycenae; there was pathos in an ivory comb three thousand years old; who had used it? And who had wept at her death?

After that he went back to the hotel, bathed and changed, and then went across to the Hilton.

He went into the bar and ordered a beer.

He was sitting alone, drinking it and reading his Greek phrase book, trying to remember simple remarks like *Hero poli* in case he was introduced to a Greek, when George Loukas came up and slapped him on the back.

'Hi, there. Lonesome?'

'Kind of,' said Patrick. Modes of speech were infectious.

'Elsie's still prettying herself. Women take so long, don't they? She's been in the beauty shop all afternoon, getting her

180

hair dyed.' He chuckled. 'She thinks I don't know that isn't her real colour. She's blonde really. Grey by now, I guess. No one's seen the true colour of her hair for years.'

'How long have you been married?'

'Fifteen years.'

'Is that all? I thought it was more.'

'No. I guess it took time to get over losing Freddie — her first husband. And Greeks don't usually marry young, you know. We have to see our sisters settled first.'

'Even in America?'

'Some do.'

'What will you drink, George?' Patrick beckoned the waiter. George demurred, Patrick over-rode him, and when George's drink had come the little man invited him to join them for dinner. After some show of reluctance Patrick accepted.

'How much longer are you staying in Athens?' he asked.

'Oh, just a few days. I'd like to make it weeks, I'm just getting to feel at home, but I guess Elsie's had enough. Isn't that right, honey?' For Elsie had appeared as they talked. Her hair certainly gleamed as black as a raven; now that Patrick thought about it, jet black hair and freckled arms did not go together in nature's scheme.

They planned to go to London, see the Tower and the Changing of the Guard, Oxford, Cambridge and Scotland. Patrick was entertained at this selectivity.

'You said you'd be visiting Reading on your trip. The biscuits haven't changed much in thirty years,' he said.

'The biscuits?' George said, looking blank.

'Cookies, you call them,' Patrick said. 'There's a factory at Reading — surely you've told George that, Elsie? The town's famous for it — and other things, of course.'

'I'd forgotten,' Elsie said.

How could she forget? The factory was a huge place, and central to the town.

They went in to dinner. George demanded steak. He was accustomed to American beef and said he was tired of all that damned mince. Patrick had steak too, and Elsie chose fish.

They drank Demestica. Afterwards George and Patrick had a meringue concoction and Elsie had fruit.

'I've got to watch my diet,' she said.

'You don't need to diet,' said Patrick. She was sturdy, big-breasted, with a broad frame but not fat; she could never be slim. He thought of how she had looked like Brunhilde in the shop in Crete, dressed in her gold-embroidered caftan.

'It's not her figure. She's diabetic,' said George, and earned a reproving frown from his wife. 'Well, honey, it's a common enough complaint. You're a good advertisement for successful therapy.' He turned to Patrick. 'Changes of food tend to upset her. She has to regulate the insulin.'

Patrick remembered the boiled sweets Elsie had produced from her bag on Mikronisos and again on the drive to Delphi; he could not remember seeing her eat one herself. Diabetics had to carry a lump of sugar or something sweet in case of a sudden coma, he seemed to recall. The pieces of the jigsaw began to fit together at last. But why? And how?

'You're very courageous about it,' he said. 'Have you had it long?'

'Oh yes — forever, you could say,' she said. 'It's too boring. Let's talk about something else.'

'We're going to Mycenae tomorrow, and Epidaurus,' said George. He pronounced it *Epidavros*, in the Greek way. 'Have you been there?'

Patrick had not.

'We're meeting up with Vera Hastings. She's planning to go along too, and it's lonesome for her on her own,' George went on. 'Why don't you join us?'

'I might at that,' said Patrick. He'd done it again: lapsed into transatlantic idiom.

IV

The helpful clerk, Kostas, who had obtained Jill's plane ticket, was on duty again when Patrick got back to the hotel. He gave Patrick two cables and a note asking him to telephone Ursula, no matter how late it was when he got in.

He went up to his room, took off his jacket, and stood on the balcony in the warm night air for a few minutes before dealing with the messages. The room opposite, where he had seen the exchange take place, was in darkness. Below, there were lights in some windows: rooms occupied by businessmen, tourists, lovers, he supposed. And haters too. How long could hatred last?

He read his cables before telephoning Ursula.

A cable from Colin said: WILL BENEFITS MISTRESS AND DAUGHTER WIFE JOYLESS BUT WEALTHY ANYWAY. A second cable, also from Colin ran: IMAGE VILLAINS IGNORANT ART EXPERT VIOLENCE. So Lucy had been taken care of; and murder featured higher on the operations list of the island gang than their thefts. He had forgotten that Gwenda had money of her own; of course, her grandfather had been a sanitary engineer, making lavatory basins, baths, and a fortune. Gwenda, the third generation, had achieved social advancement by dint of her expensive education and judicious marriage.

He lifted the telephone and asked for Ursula's number. She answered at once.

'Patrick?' Her voice was clipped, the tone urgent.

'Yes. Sorry to be so late.'

'Never mind. You realize the importance of what we discussed today? The discrepancy? Vera Hastings will have noticed it too, if she thinks about it.'

'Yes. I've been thinking about that. She started to say something at Delphi and then changed her mind. Perhaps she wasn't sure if she remembered accurately.'

'There's something else. Two more things. When did Elsie say her husband was killed?'

'In 1941. Yes, I'm sure of that.'

'And when did she go to Africa? You said she served there.'

They had discussed Elsie's war-time career after Ursula's disclosure that she had been an officer in the same service.

'She was married there,' said Patrick. 'What are you getting at? She was only married a few weeks.'

Ursula told him.

'And there's something else,' she said. 'Something I noticed in Challika after you left. Some words in Greek scratched on the stone inside that old pill-box on the headland.' She repeated what they said. 'But how was it done? And why?'

'I've got an idea about how,' said Patrick heavily. 'I don't know why.'

'Are you going to the police?'

'I haven't any proof. What can they do? It's all surmise even with what you've told me. But I've got a plan.'

'Yes?'

'I need some help. Vera is going to Mycenae and Epidaurus tomorrow. So are the Loukases. She could be in danger, if she says anything to Elsie. I'm going too — as a bodyguard, and I want to set something up, but I can't do it alone. Would you come too?'

'What do you mean to do?'

'It needs more thought, but roughly, this—' He began to explain.

'Yes,' she said, when he had done. 'It might work. I'll help, and so will a friend of mine, Nikos Hadzmichalis. We'll be with you for breakfast.'

V

They arrived at half-past seven and all three hatched their plan in the hotel dining-room over coffee, rolls and apricot jam.

Nikos spoke excellent English; he had lived in London for several years but never left Greece now. He did not have to explain why. He was an engineer and his skill was valuable. He had warm brown eyes which belied the austerity of his face with its aquiline nose; his profile could have come from a Greek vase, except that the faces on them were all youthful. There was no time now to find out his history or how he and Ursula had met. It was sufficient that he was a man of authority; Patrick was reassured when Nikos agreed with his judgement that there was not enough, yet, to tell the police.

'I hope we've thought of everything,' he said, with some diffidence, when they had gone over their plans thoroughly.

'I think so, Dr Grant,' said Nikos.

'And remember, when we meet at Epidaurus, you two don't know each other,' said Ursula to the men.

'If this doesn't work, we'll think up another scheme,' said Nikos. 'Today we must play for safety. I wish we could prevent this Mrs Hastings from taking the trip.'

So did Patrick, but they did not know how to get hold of her, except possibly through the Loukases, and that must not be done.

'Well, I'd better go,' said Patrick. 'I must get to the coach terminal before the others.' It was just round the corner; the invaluable Kostas had already made out his ticket.

'Here's a torch, for Mycenae,' said Nikos, handing Patrick a small, neat pocket one. 'You'll need it. The tours don't spend long there, but don't fret when your guide takes you away. Ursula and I will take you back when this is all over.'

Patrick left them drinking more coffee. They were going in Nikos's car; it would be quicker, and the people in the coach would not see them until the time for their meeting. He marvelled at them as he walked out of the dining room; they were like a couple who had been happily married for years, giving out a united strength, yet both had an aura of youthful excitement. Had they some permanent future arranged? He did not think so, from Ursula's remarks about the vagueness of her plans; perhaps such a thing was impossible.

In the road he stopped at a kiosk and bought several small packets of boiled sweets, which he put in his pocket. Then he walked quickly along the street to where a row of coaches was drawn up outside the tour offices. Soon more coaches bringing tourists from hotels all over Athens would converge here, and the passengers would be sorted into the right buses for their various destinations. There was always someone who misunderstood or got muddled, took the wrong coach, or was rude to the guide; yet somehow the couriers stayed patient throughout.

Vera Hastings arrived soon after Patrick, in a taxi. She paid it off, then stood looking rather bemused on the pavement in a crowd of Swedes all going to Hydra. Patrick approached her.

'Hullo,' he said. 'You're going to Mycenae and Epidaurus, aren't you? Shall we sit together?'

'Oh, that would be nice. The Loukases are coming too. Did you know?' she said.

'Yes, indeed. They told me last night.'

Even so early in the day, plump Vera Hastings was flushed and heated. Patrick, who wore a linen jacket because he needed its pockets, not for warmth, patted the torch, safely in his pocket; in another were the sweets, and a paperback copy of *The Lion's Gate*. He took reading matter about with him wherever he went as another man would cigarettes.

'I think this is our coach,' he said, taking Vera's arm and leading her through the Swedes who divided for them like the Red Sea before Moses. A group of Germans blocked the way next, and Patrick would not be baulked nor go round, when they did not move.

Bitte,' he said, tapping a stout man. *'Bitte schön.'* He forged a path, and checked their destination with a slim lad who stood by the coach door holding a list, although the vehicle was clearly labelled.

'Your name, sir, please?' The youth searched on his list and eventually passed them in. They picked a seat near the front and had been there for almost ten minutes before the Loukases arrived. By then the coach was filling up.

Patrick saw a middle-aged man in a flowered shirt eagerly join a younger one who gave him a sharp, calculating glance, then brightened; well, their day was made already.

Elsie and George had to sit near the rear of the coach. When it moved off at last, Patrick relaxed; there was nothing to do now but wait. Meanwhile he might as well enjoy the trip.

They stopped at Corinth, where the coach drew up outside a sprawling modern *kafenion* and the passengers walked back to the bridge spanning the canal. The sheer rent in the earth, with its steep red sides and the brilliant blue of the sky above, was a dramatic sight, marred by one of the ubiquitous signs proclaiming the anniversary of the events of 1967 strung across the ravine in an eye-catching position. After observing the scene from both sides of the bridge the party trooped back to the *kafenion* for refreshments. It was a bad moment for Patrick when Vera Hastings went off to the cloakroom; he could not follow her there. But Elsie was sitting at a table with George drinking coffee. They had seen the canal before, they said, when they visited George's cousins.

From Corinth they went on through beautiful rolling scenery among groves of orange trees and lemons, and little white villages perched on the hills. Mrs Hastings fell asleep.

One of the first things Patrick saw when the coach stopped at Epidaurus was Nikos's car; he recognized it with relief. He had not seen it pass the coach, for Vera was on the window side. There was no sign of Ursula or of Nikos, but that was the plan. They were to be waiting, strategically positioned, in the theatre, having carried out a small experiment.

The beauty of the setting took Patrick by surprise; he almost forgot his grim mission as he looked across to the distant mountains. Here it was verdant and green; no doubt the natural attributes of the place helped Asclepius with his cures. Their guide led them along past the stadium, tiny by comparison with the vast area of Delphi, and on to the Tholos, where they learned of the snake-pit remedy; drastic indeed. After a short time in the museum, where Elsie Loukas found the ancient surgical instruments interesting, they wandered on towards the theatre. She had been a dental nurse when George and she met, Patrick remembered; such things would hold a professional appeal for her. Learning to give herself insulin injections must have been easier for her than for a lay person. She would have an expert knowledge of anatomy, if she were a fully-trained nurse.

She was walking along beside him and Vera now; George had gone on ahead and was filming the three of them as they approached. He retreated steadily as they advanced, holding the camera as it turned; behind him, as they reached the limits of the theatre, Patrick saw Ursula's white head. She and Nikos were standing at the foot of the great semi-circular range of tiered seats. One other group of tourists with their guide were standing in a cluster on the stage; a few people on their own moved among the seats or wandered about, staring at the great theatre in its tranquil surroundings. The guide began to tell them about the annual drama festival held here; what a wonderful thing to attend, thought Patrick. But he was in the midst of a contemporary drama, and must forget Euripides for it was time to play his part.

'Why look! There's Ursula Norris,' he cried, striking, as Ursula told him later, an attitude. 'You met her on the journey to Athens, Vera. Do you remember?'

'Yes — oh, how nice.' Vera, always prim, was nevertheless pleased.

'And you met her in Crete,' Patrick reminded George and Elsie.

'Patrick! What a lovely surprise!' exclaimed Ursula, and to his amazement, kissed him warmly. She gave his arm a little squeeze and breathed into his ear, 'It's fine.' So their test had worked. 'And Mr and Mrs Loukas,' she went on, with almost no pause. 'May I introduce Nikos Hadzimichalis?'

Nikos, looking bashful, stepped forward.

'He speaks very little English,' said Ursula.

Patrick blinked. This was new. What had they been plotting without him? But he seized the opportunity, put out his hand, and said firmly, '*Hero poli.*'

'How are you?' said Nikos, with an affected thick accent, gripping his hand.

George immediately broke into rapid Greek; soon the two men were chattering away, sounding excited; they could only be discussing trivialities yet their voices and gestures might lead the observer to suppose they were arguing about life and death, such was the Greek manner of conversation.

Life and death.

Vera Hastings was talking to Ursula. Nikos said something to George, who answered, '*Nai, nai,*' in vehement tones, and the two began to ascend an aisle dividing the blocks of seats; while they climbed they continued to talk and gesticulate. Patrick moved close to Vera; Ursula stood on her other side; Elsie faced the three of them, a little apart. Only words could be used as weapons here, before so many possible witnesses, but the manoeuvre had psychological importance. The guide, with the rest of the group had crossed the stage to the further side and was addressing them.

Nikos and George had reached a considerable height now; Patrick glanced up, saw Nikos make a quick gesture to George for silence, and point below. It was time to begin.

'How odd that you three ladies were all in the Wrens during the war, yet never met,' he said.

Elsie's head shot up.

'Were you, too?' she asked Ursula.

'Yes. I was an administrative officer,' Ursula said. 'What were you?'

'A clerk,' said Elsie.

'Oh — a writer, do you mean?' Vera asked.

'You left under a cloud, didn't you?' Patrick said.

Elsie had stiffened. Her eyes looked very black, the pupils dilated.

'I was thinking about that,' said Vera, now playing her part as if she had rehearsed it. 'Why were you afraid of being court-martialled? You mentioned it at Delphi. Wrens never were. We used to joke about it. That's right, isn't it?' she appealed to Ursula.

'Perfectly correct,' said Ursula. 'And there were no Wrens in North Africa until 1942. I worked on the scheme for sending out the first group.'

'You were not in the British Forces at all,' said Patrick, but he said it in German. Vera looked bewildered, Ursula determined, and Elsie, who seemed now to be surrounded by the others in a threatening group, looked hunted.

'I don't speak German,' she said, in English.

'I think you do,' said Patrick. 'You understood it in a shop in Crete and you're understanding me now.' No one knew if George understood German, so the conversation must go on in English, and he switched languages. 'What's that tune? How does it go? Beethoven wrote it. He was another German. *Für Elise*. For Elsie.' And he hummed the opening notes. 'You knew Felix Lomax, didn't you? You met him in Venice and he recognized you, in spite of your dyed hair. What had you done, Elise, that made him follow you to Crete, and was so terrible that you killed him to prevent George learning about it?'

Vera was looking at him in horror, quite uncomprehending. But Elsie rallied.

'You must be mad,' she said to Patrick and pushed past him. 'We're missing the guide's talk.' And she walked away from them towards the rest of the group.

'She's cool, you have to admit,' said Patrick, looking after her.

'What — what's going on?' asked Vera. She looked shocked.

'I wonder if it worked,' said Ursula. She and Patrick were both looking up at Nikos and George, who were now talking together, Nikos with a hand on George's arm. 'I think so,' she said. 'Anyway, we must get you out of this, Vera. You must come back with Nikos and me. I'll explain in the car. It's all right, really it is. But you mustn't stay with the tour.' She looked at Patrick. 'She'll hardly tackle all of us, but she'll be desperate now, Won't you come too?'

He shook his head.

'No. I'm staying with George,' he said. 'But please go with Ursula, Vera. I'll tell the guide you felt ill.'

And indeed she had gone rather pale.

'Felix Lomas was that friend of Lucy Amberley's. The one who died,' she said.

'You knew him?' Patrick asked.

'Oh yes,' said Vera. 'He came into the bank with her once. And I read about his accident in the *Athens News*.' She stared at Patrick and then looked over at the group of tourists, in the midst of whom stood Elsie, apparently intent on the guide's discourse. 'But—?' her voice trailed away.

'We don't know the whole story. Ursula will tell you what we think happened,' Patrick said. 'Now, please will you do as we ask? You could be in danger, because you were a genuine Wren and you know that Elsie was not.'

The group was moving off now towards the coach, Elsie on the heels of the guide. George and Nikos were coming down the steps between the tiered seats back to the stage, in silence; Nikos, a pace behind the other man, nodded at Ursula and Patrick. Owing to the remarkable acoustics of Polyclitus's enormous auditorium they had heard every syllable of what had been said below them; and Elsie, because she had not read about this nor witnessed the guide's paper-tearing demonstration, did not know what had happened.

George was ashen under his normal olive colour; when he looked at Patrick there was agony in his eyes.

'Niko, I'm taking Vera to the car,' said Ursula. 'You come when you're ready.'

'Yes.' Nikos had time to give her a warm look; then he spoke urgently to George in a low voice. The two women went off together and Patrick walked along behind the two Greeks; Nikos seemed to be advising George, who looked as if a thunderbolt from Jupiter himself had struck him, and no wonder.

There was someone following along behind Patrick. It was not Elsie; she was ahead with the rest of the tour. He glanced over his shoulder and was astounded to see Inspector Manolakis, last seen in Crete, wearing tourist clothes and huge dark glasses. He opened his mouth to speak, but Manolakis shook his head very slightly and went on walking.

Patrick took his cue and looked away. The policeman had been up in the auditorium and heard the whole thing too.

VI

George followed Elsie into the coach and they took their former seat, at the rear. Patrick hung back so that he was one of the last to board; he could not bear to look at George, whom he had just destroyed. He resumed his seat.

A figure loomed beside him and took the vacant place; it was Manolakis. The guide cast them an anguished look; she was a plump woman of about forty, upset already because her flock had got separated in the theatre, and now she had exchanged a British lady for a policeman in plain clothes. She feared for her job and described the next stage of their journey, which would take them to Nauplia for lunch, with extra diligence in several languages on her inter-com.

'May I introduce myself? My name is Dimitris Manolakis and I am on holiday for a few days in Athens. I am a bank clerk,' said the inspector suavely. 'I missed my own coach, so the guide kindly said I was to take this place. You are English, sir?'

'Yes, from Oxford. You speak very good English, *Kirie* Manolaki,' said Patrick, hoping he had used the vocative correctly and scored a point thereby.

'I like to practise,' said the other with calm.

And he did, for the whole journey to Nauplia, talking about trivialities and asking precise questions about grammar every few minutes. Patrick wondered what Elsie and George were discussing. Or were they silent? He felt the packets of sweets in his pocket. It had been wise to bring them, but they wouldn't be needed now. No one was going into an insulin coma. But Elsie might have contrived to lead Vera apart from the rest; somehow she had done this to Felix, so that if he had screamed he had not been heard.

They had lunch in a large, modern hotel overlooking the sea at long tables especially laid up for the party.

'It's marvellous how the hotels cope with all these tourists,' Patrick said to Manolakis as they entered the hotel and were greeted by flagging but still smiling waiters.

'Cope? Cope? What is that, please? A bishop's robings, yes?' asked Manolakis.

Patrick patiently explained the verb.

'Ah yes. I remember that.' Manolakis took a small book from his pocket and wrote in it. He passed it to Patrick who hoped to read a cryptic message therein, but all he saw was a crabbed script and the words *cope, manage*, with a Greek word alongside.

'Quite right,' he sighed. He felt the initiative had gone from him, but at least Vera was safe. He went into the men's room.

George was there. He was washing his face with cold water. Patrick decided that the best course was to behave as if he did not know George had overheard the scene in the theatre, unless George himself did otherwise.

'I felt a bit sick in the coach,' said George. He looked at Patrick pleadingly. 'Sit with us at lunch, won't you?'

But it was impossible. Elsie had already secured places for herself and George among strangers. Manolakis, too, had taken a seat between one of the queers who had met on the coach and were now the happiest of men, and a stout Swedish woman. He looked prim, just like a rather subservient bank clerk. Patrick spared time to admire his impersonation; he must be a first-class policeman, too, for his presence here was by no means coincidence. He hadn't been satisfied, in Challika, about Felix. The smell of things, Colin called it; a copper's hunch. Patrick's own tendency to develop it had led Colin to suggest he changed his career before now.

The only place left for Patrick was on the far side of the two homosexuals, next to the elder one, with a youngish German woman on his other side. He ignored the man; in any case he had no choice, for the other was intent on charming his new friend. Patrick talked to the German woman in her own tongue throughout the meal. He found that she was travelling alone, so he invited her to sit in Vera's place and flirted with her mildly all the way to Mycenae. Manolakis was obliged to sit with her former travelling companion, a Belgian lady who spoke no Greek and very little English. The inspector did not seem to include French among his accomplishments, and they travelled in silence.

The guide lectured them diligently over the loudspeaker, describing the citadel and the tombs. She gave her spiel in English, French and German. When they reached Mycenae and got out of the coach the atmosphere was at once totally different from that of Epidaurus; this was a place of tragedy, and the aura of menace clung here still. The ruins brooded over the surrounding plain and there was a sense of doom in the air.

Schliemann had excavated this place: a German archaeologist. Patrick's thoughts flew off at a tangent, and he disciplined them sternly back to the present while the guide talked about the Treasury of Atreus, once thought to be the burial place of Agamemnon but in fact older still. They went into the enormous beehive tomb and stood awed inside. Manolakis was close to Patrick now; so were Elsie and George. The guide pointed out the entrance to the smaller burial chamber beyond the first great tomb, and a number of people filed through it.

Patrick stepped through the entrance. Now the reason why Nikos had given him the torch became clear; he stood on a rough earth floor in total darkness. Here and there people lit cigarette lighters or struck matches, and wan lights flickered in the gloom. Patrick moved further in, the torch in his hand. Someone pressed against him, and he moved on slowly; how big was this place? Sweat sprang out on his brow. Damn it, she could jab a needle into him now and no one would know what was wrong with him. Why hadn't he told Manolakis about the insulin? He wouldn't scream: of course he wouldn't. Britons didn't scream if they were being injected with death before thirty strangers. How quickly would it take effect? He licked his dry lips. If only she could be caught in the attempt; that was what he had hoped for.

He felt a movement behind him, very close, and swung round suddenly, switching on his torch, the beam high. It lighted Elsie's face as she stood next to him. She blinked and stepped backwards and at the same moment he felt a sharp pain in his hand. There was a clatter, and an exclamation. Elsie had dropped her handbag.

In a second there was a bustle as people helped her to gather up her dropped belongings; Patrick withdrew towards the outer tomb trying to keep calm; his hand seemed to be damaged, but it had not felt like the thrust of a hypodermic.

Manolakis was suddenly beside him, leading him out into the fresh air, where Patrick, to his surprise, found that the palm of his left hand was bleeding.

'You are all right,' Manolakis told him firmly.

'Yes, of course I am,' said Patrick indignantly. Did the fellow think he would pass out at the sight of his own blood? He mopped at it with his large white linen handkerchief, which he then wrapped round the wound. It was a nasty cut, the type that bleeds freely, but not serious enough to require stitching. Manolakis glanced round. No one seemed to be watching them; those who were not helping Elsie with her possessions were photographing the entrance to the tomb, or each other. The policeman slipped something out of his pocket. It, too, appeared to be a white linen handkerchief, but as he unwrapped it and held it in his palm for Patrick to see, he revealed a slim stiletto knife. He wrapped it up again and replaced it in his pocket, then led Patrick on towards the citadel where their guide was impatiently waiting, looking at her watch. The schedule was tight and if the tourists strayed, so did her timetable.

'Try not to let her see you were hurt. She thinks she has lost the knife in the tomb. She will be happy to leave it there,' said the inspector in a soft murmur.

'It's all right. It's not serious,' said Patrick. His relief at finding he had merely avoided a stabbing, not an injection, was profound. He was stupid to have thought she would try that, though; how could she load a syringe in the dark, much less press it home?

'We'll move a little away. Then we can see if we must get you something to — to' his English deserted Manolakis as he sought for the word for a dressing. 'To stop blood,' he said firmly. 'It is some hours till we reach Athens.'

It would be a pity if he bled quietly to death in the coach while they waited for more evidence against Elsie, thought Patrick, melodramatically. Was this not enough? But it wasn't; of course not. Specific proof of the crime against Felix was what they wanted.

The guide was talking about Schliemann's finds and instructing her hearers to look at them in the Archaeological Museum. She frowned as Manolakis, talking about Orestes, led Patrick off to the top of the acropolis. Here they were able to inspect the damage; it was not at all severe, and some sticking plaster would soon hold the sides of the small wound together, but they had none.

'One of the ladies will have some, in her handbag,' said Manolakis. 'Or the coach driver.'

'We don't want Elsie Loukas to see, though. It's all right, it's stopping,' said Patrick. He wrapped his handkerchief round it more tightly; Manolakis tied it in position. 'I'll put my hand in my pocket, then it won't show,' he said. What a fuss.

'It is clean. No germs,' said Manolakis earnestly.

Fancy knowing the word; Patrick did not know the equivalent in either French or German.

'Your English is getting better every minute,' he said.

They sat together in the coach returning to Athens, to the chagrin of the German woman whose acquaintance Patrick had been so busily cultivating. On Manolakis's advice Patrick tucked his hand under the lapel of his jacket in a Napoleonic manner, to raise it and thus help the bleeding to stop.

'She's a diabetic, Elsie Loukas,' he informed the policeman. 'I think if you inject a healthy person with insulin they go into a coma.'

'I think you speak truth,' said Manolakis. 'And it is hard to find in the dead one, unless you look for it — how do you say it — because you believe it is there. There is a new test in recent years.'

'So if she put Felix Lomax in the sea unconscious, he'd be sure to drown,' said Patrick. 'And it would seem to be an accident.'

'It would seem to be.' Manolakis repeated the intricate construction, docketing it away in his mind for future use, Patrick was sure.

'You suspected this?' he asked.

'I knew it was not as easy as it would seem to be,' said Manolakis, triumphantly. 'But there is no proof.'

'Her first husband,' said Patrick, thinking aloud. 'She said he was an archaeologist, killed in Crete. She was posing as British, so of course that meant her husband was British too. If he was German—' his thoughts went back to Schliemann. German archaeologists had been interested in Mikronisos before the war. 'His name was Freddie. That may have been Friedrich. She just changed her own name round, after all. If you could discover who he was—? I expect it was true that he was killed in Crete, but by the British or the Greeks. It would be difficult to trace him.' He told Manolakis what Elsie had said about Mikronisos. 'There might be records of archaeologists interested in the island,' he suggested.

'We would need help from Germany,' said Manolakis. 'It could be tried. It would not be quick.' And even if something were found, by then the Loukases would have left Greece.

Felix could be exhumed and his remains tested for insulin, but even if it were found where was the link with Elsie? Unless they could force her to tell them, how would it ever be known? And George! What about George? In all their theorising they had forgotten him.

'I think she does not realize that her husband heard you, at *Epidavros*,' said Manolakis thoughtfully. 'I would not like it if I had in error married myself to one who had killed my people.' He meditated briefly. 'We younger ones are not so bitter, it is true. But the older men — like Loukas — it is different.'

Manolakis was perhaps a year or two younger than Patrick; quite old enough to remember the war and what had happened in Crete; he might have run errands for the *andartes*. He could have had relatives who were massacred.

What would George do? Did he believe what he had heard?

The coach stopped at old Corinth on the way back, and Patrick regretted his inability to appreciate the scene of St. Paul's activities. Manolakis had resumed his bank clerk role and even asked questions of the guide, which unnerved her since she was well aware of his true identity. Everyone was tired by this time, and most people would have preferred to drive straight back to Athens without stopping, as they did, for more refreshments on the toll road. Elsie disappeared into the cloakroom, and Manolakis spoke to one of the *kafenion* assistants who produced a first-aid box. The policeman took it into the men's room, bidding Patrick follow. Here he carried out a neat cleaning-up operation on Patrick's hand, bathing it and securing the wound with gauze and plaster. The job was just complete when George came out of one of the cubicles. He looked at Patrick's hand, and at the bloodstained handkerchief which lay on the washbasin beside him, but he made no comment.

'That's fine. Thanks,' said Patrick in a bright voice to the inspector. He dropped the handkerchief into a waste-bin; it was of no further use to him. Then he went out of the cloakroom leaving the two Greeks together. Perhaps Manolakis would say something to George. But he followed Patrick, clearly having maintained his *incognito*. When George reappeared all three started to admire the sunset.

Elsie did not return until just before the coach left. She was pale but looked composed.

'Ah — there you are, honey,' said George, going up to her. He seemed better himself now; the grey, pinched look had gone from his face and his voice was normal as he greeted his wife. It was a brave effort, for Greeks are not good dissemblers. The two were dropped at the Hilton on the way in to the centre of Athens; Manolakis left the coach when it stopped outside another hotel, but with no more than a casual goodbye.

Patrick knew that they would meet again shortly, and he had just entered his own hotel, having paused to buy *The Times* on the way, when Manolakis followed him through the doors.

VII

There was a message for Patrick from the Athens police, who wanted to speak to him. Well, they must wait. There was also a cable from Colin which said: WIFE UNIMPEACHABLE ALIBI PAST FORTNIGHT MARRIAGE GUIDING AND MORAL REARMAMENT. So that was how Gwenda had been occupied recently. Had she known about Felix's new will before his death? It did not matter now. There was a letter, too, from England, in an unknown hand. Probably from Jeremy or Celia, thought Patrick, bemoaning what had happened at the end of their holiday.

'Let's have a drink,' he said to Manolakis.

'Are you not going to read your letter?' asked the inspector when they were sitting in the bar with their ouzos.

It was really a most refreshing drink, thought Patrick, watching the liquid turn cloudy as he added some water; he had long ago stopped finding its flavour like cough syrup.

'I'll just see who it's from,' he said, and ripped the envelope open. The writing was large and clear; he glanced at the signature and then at the address which headed the first page. It was a long letter.

'It's from Gwenda Lomax,' he said.

'The widow?'

'Yes.' Patrick had begun to read intently. 'Good heavens,' he said. 'It's all here — what we want. The motive, I mean.'

Gwenda had telephoned Jane, whom she knew slightly, to find out where Patrick was staying in Crete and had learned of his move to Athens. She was not satisfied about the manner of Felix's death, but did not want to cause a disturbance by asking for further enquiries without adequate grounds. She could think of no reason why Felix should have gone to Crete so suddenly unless he had stumbled upon some ghost from the past, and the one thing that had haunted him through all the years of their marriage had been the terrible death of a friend of his, during the war. She wanted Patrick to make some judicious investigations, and if he felt there was cause, take up the matter with the police again.

Felix had been in a German hospital in North Africa after his capture, wounded. In the next bed was a friend of his, Tom Lacey, wounded more seriously but recovering. Both officers had been receiving excellent care, like every patient; the German doctors and nurses were above the conflict. It was chance that Tom and Felix were together, for Tom had served in Crete; they were not in the same regiment.

One night, when most of the men in the ward were asleep, a nurse had approached Tom and said it was time for his shot. He'd had it, said Tom. Another had been ordered, said the nurse. She had then injected Tom in the arm and had gone away. She had been on the ward for some time, and her name was Elise. The men did not know her surname, but she was a widow.

Felix had fallen asleep and woken to hear terrible screams coming from Tom, who had died in agony. Elise had not been seen again; she had been found unfit to serve at the front; and had been sent home. Felix had not let the matter rest there; he was sure the nurse, whose husband had been killed in Crete, had injected Tom with some fatal substance, as an act of vengeance. He had pursued the matter, after the war, but with no result. Although he had given up mentioning it,

Gwenda knew that he had never forgotten it. He had tried to trace the nurse himself when official methods had proved unsuccessful but at last had had to give up, hoping retribution had caught up with her anyway.

Patrick silently handed Manolakis the letter. The Greek read it slowly and painstakingly, once or twice asking for explanations.

'So that is it,' he said.

'She found security in America, I suppose. And George has money,' said Patrick. What a horrible story. What had Felix tried to do? He had not been clever enough to outwit Elise, that was certain. He had stopped thinking of her as Elsie already.

'She may have done other things, also,' said Manolakis. 'In Germany, later. Things her own countrymen would not like. We will have to discover. They may want her themselves.'

War crimes. It was possible. And poor George was the fall guy. What about his *philotimo* now?

Manolakis said he would like to have the letter photo-copied. Might he take it away, and bring it back in an hour or so? Patrick asked if he was going to bring the matter to the attention of the Athens police, and he said not immediately; first he would attempt to trace Elsie's true identity by finding out the name of her archaeologist husband. When there was more to go on, then, if necessary, the Lomax case would be re-opened. He was here on his own initiative, not officially.

'You come back to Crete. You stay with me. I have a nice house, a nice wife, nice children — and a sister,' said Manolakis. 'We have many nice talks about all this trouble and you teach me English.'

His was slipping; Patrick knew the feeling; after a day spent speaking another language suddenly the effort became too much when one grew tired, and the simplest phrase eluded one.

'Thank you,' he said. What a pleasant idea, especially the sister. But Greeks guarded their sisters' virtue jealously. 'I'll see,' he said.

Manolakis went off with the letter and he went up to his room where he telephoned the police, who said they would like to see him, but the next morning would do. Then he telephoned Ursula.

He learned that she and Nikos had taken a very distressed Vera back to her family. She had agreed to say nothing to her daughter or son-in-law until the next day, but the young people did not seem satisfied with the tale she had spun about feeling unwell. They did remember, however, that she had mentioned travelling out with Ursula, and her son-in-law knew Nikos by repute, which had been some reassurance to them. Vera was not cut out for involvement in melodrama, said Ursula; even her naval career had been spent very safely in Scotland in some paymaster's department.

Patrick said that a letter had come from Gwenda which made everything clear, though it proved nothing. It was arranged that Ursula and Nikos would have dinner with him in the hotel and learn what had happened after they parted that morning at Epidaurus.

There was a lot to tell them, Patrick thought, when they had rung off. He looked ruefully at his hand, which throbbed slightly; he hoped Manolakis was right about germs.

Ursula did not even know that Manolakis had come over from Crete.

VIII

'So Gwenda turned up trumps in the end,' said Ursula, and then had to explain this idiom to Nikos and Dimitris Manolakis. The policeman had returned with the letter just as Ursula and Nikos arrived, and had been persuaded to join them for dinner.

'Yes.' Patrick had to admit that Gwenda's sense of duty had triumphed. Perhaps she was not so bad really; just wrong for Felix; inappropriate pairing.

They had finished an excellent meal and were sitting in comfortable chairs in a corner of the lounge going over the story. Manolakis showed them photographs of the stiletto which Elsie had dropped in the tomb; he had already taken it to some official department for finger-printing; it would help trace Elsie's true identity if she were wanted in Germany. The dagger was very old, the handle beautifully wrought and chased with an intricate design; the men in the police department had exclaimed over it and would refer it to experts. They were sure it was priceless, and Manolakis thought it must be some trophy Elsie's husband had found in one of his digs.

'She could be extradited, I expect,' said Patrick.

Manolakis knew that her first husband had been to Mikronisos; Patrick wondered how much he knew about the more recent events on the island: just what had been reported in the papers, or, by now, the details?

'Your holiday is not giving you rest,' the policeman said. 'Remember my words.'

Patrick laughed and said he would do so. Manolakis then made his excuses and left them.

'What a nice man,' said Ursula. 'I remember liking him before, when he had that coffee with us in Challika.'

'He is clever,' said Nikos.

'Is your hand really all right?' Ursula asked.

'Yes — the trouble was trying to conceal it,' said Patrick. 'I suppose it was stupid to think she'd try something with insulin. She couldn't in a place like that.'

'Still — you were prepared,' said Nikos. 'She was versatile.'

'She couldn't have hoped to get away with stabbing you, though,' said Ursula. Suppose the knife had plunged into Patrick's heart or lungs?

'I don't know. If I hadn't yelled, and if she'd done it when I was out of the way — so that no one stumbled over me. And if I wasn't missed straight away—' Patrick's voice trailed off. 'She didn't know who Manolakis was. She might have fobbed George off.'

'It was a long shot,' said Ursula, and had to explain that one to Nikos.

Patrick wondered what would happen to both of them. There they sat, happy together, the position perfectly clear, yet he felt it was a transitory time for them.

Nikos ordered more coffee, and before it arrived Patrick was called to the telephone. He was gone some time, and when he returned his face was grave.

'What's happened? It's not Vera?' asked Ursula.

'No. That was George,' said Patrick. 'He wanted to ask about my hand. He noticed it was cut when we stopped on the way back, and he'd discovered an antique stiletto which Elsie used as a paper knife and took everywhere with her was missing.'

'She'd never get through an airport frisking with that thing,' said Ursula. 'I suppose she packed it in her suitcase. Go on.' For Patrick clearly had more to tell.

'He'd seen a letter,' Patrick said. 'A photocopy. A messenger brought it, he said.' Had Manolakis gone there himself? Patrick felt he was being incoherent, where George on the telephone had been perfectly clear.

'Elsie's not very well. She's feeling thirsty and has a headache,' he said. 'They're leaving Athens early tomorrow and flying to Rome. George thinks she's suffering from the heat, so he's hiring a car and taking her up into the mountains. They'll go to some small village.' He looked at the other two. 'He doesn't speak French or Italian, he said, and "of course you know that Elsie speaks no German, so if she falls ill in a village where there is no doctor it would be difficult." That's just what he said, his very words,' said Patrick.

There was a silence.

'Insulin looks like water,' said Ursula at last. 'If she doesn't get the right dose — if it's diluted—' she did not finish.

'Yes,' said Patrick.

'He means to do it?' Ursula's voice was shaky.

'I think he's begun already,' said Patrick. 'But he won't let it happen in Greece. I think he means to take her back to where she came from.'

PART SIX:
FRIDAY

CRETE

I

Two days later Patrick flew to Heraklion.

He had spent some time with the Athens police on Thursday. They had a strong lead to the identity of Kamal; according to the London information it seemed as if the grave had been found by chance. The men were really involved with arms smuggling; they brought shipments from various sources and hid them in a cave on Mikronisos before sending them on to their ultimate destination. Once a small bomb had gone off by accident, exposing the side of a stone coffin and incidentally killing one of the gang, whose body had now been found on the island.

Kamal, who was pretending to be interested in the project of building a hotel on the island in order to roam freely over it, had realized the value of the unexpected find. Help from Crete had been recruited; one of Kamal's accomplices had once worked as an unskilled labourer on an official dig there and knew of a woman who had helped with more expert work and some vase repairs. Her son had been traced and persuaded to join them, bringing her too. He had been in prison already for fraud and was easy to enlist. All this Arthur Winterton had revealed before he died, hoping for clemency if he told what he knew. But Yannis had feared the advent of an inquisitive godfather from England who might ask too many questions and who knew about the ancient remains. The car of the friend he was to travel with had been wrecked in an effort to keep him away when he wrote to say he was coming; then the man himself had died.

'My God,' cried Patrick, when this was disclosed. 'They smashed up my car to stop us?'

'To delay you. They were getting out of the antiques business,' said the Greek police officer. 'They'd come to the end of one grave and they didn't know there might be others. The arms business was more in their line, but our officials were thinking it was time plans for the hotel took more definite shape. It looked as if questions would soon be asked, and Kamal meant to operate from some other base. Scotland Yard has found two of the minor members of the organization. Arthur Winterton committed suicide. When the police let him go on bail he was afraid that the gang would kill him because he had told so much; he knew they were merciless. He had not expected to be released like that. Dermott Murcott surprised them in the cave, cleaning up the last of their finds. He had to be silenced. They knocked him out and then took him back up the cliff and threw him over so that he would be found some distance away.'

'I see,' said Patrick. He could not get over the wanton destruction of his car. What a nerve!

'Your friends in London will tell you, when you see them. The good Inspector Smithers.' The Greek officer smiled. 'We are very grateful to you, Dr Grant. We will trace the men, I hope. We do not want another illegal arms business operating from our soil. I hope you will have no trouble replacing your car.'

'Oh — the insurance will pay, I suppose.' By the time he got home they might have made up their minds about the amount due. He would have to decide what sort of car to get; not another Rover, he thought: something a little more sporty, perhaps.

He parted cordially from the policemen, who would now never need the cigarette-stub so carefully preserved. Then, with Ursula, he went to see Vera Hastings. They told her most of the story, but not the terrible revenge which George would exact. Vera was left assuming that Inspector Manolakis would wind the affair up in a few days; she promised to keep her own counsel meanwhile. Manolakis would, eventually, discover what happened, Patrick was sure.

The Loukases had checked out from the Hilton that morning; Mrs Loukas had not seemed well; she complained of a severe headache and thirst, Patrick was told when he telephoned the hotel to ask about them.

In the evening he had dined at Tourcolimanos with Ursula and Nikos; he would see them again on his way home to England and they would make the promised return visit to Mycenae.

And now he was back in Crete. He had hired a car at the airport, and he drove straight to Ai Saranda. The old men he had met before were at the *kafenion*, and welcomed him as a friend but they were still evasive. Ilena was back in the village, they said, and sent him to see her, with an interpreter.

She was very tense and her manner was reserved, but she was shocked and distressed to hear of Alec's death. She had been away from Crete on a long visit but was back now for good and glad to be home. Yannis was not with her; she did not know where he was exactly, she thought it might be Beirut. But he was a good son and would see her provided for. Patrick wondered how Yannis had managed to persuade her to go to Mikronisos; he must have spun her some tale and convinced her that he was turning over a new leaf. Once on the island she would have found it impossible to get away.

He did not press her, nor did he offer to visit her again before leaving Crete. He would protect her better by keeping away.

It seemed very peaceful in Challika when he returned there. The *Psyche* was moored at her usual berth and Spiro was swabbing her deck. Patrick wondered how Yannis had managed to involve Spiro in his nefarious doings. Perhaps Spiro had simply been trying to make enough money to marry Sophia, but poor Jill had been duped. He evidently hoped to bluff it out; if Yannis stayed free he would probably get away with it.

He would have to decide where to stay. On the whole it might be prudent not to risk the temptations of Manolakis's sister. While he thought about it, he parked close to the Hermes, where he had stayed before, and walked over to the pillbox on the headland. There, as Ursula had said, was scratched on the stones, inside, the sentence which meant 'The German woman Elise has—' and then ended, incomplete. Patrick ran his fingers over the Greek script. He was thus engaged when he heard a footfall and turned to see Dimitris Manolakis standing beside him.

'But how?' Patrick asked.

'We'll never know,' said Manolakis. 'Perhaps she saw him coming up the cliff — they may have met by chance. Perhaps she had agreed to meet him here.'

So Manolakis knew Felix had arrived by boat. How much did he know about the *Psyche* and her journeys? He must have learned the whole story of Mikronisos by this time. What about poor little Sophia from the shop?

'She struck him, perhaps. She knew, perhaps, just where to hit. When he fell later, it would seem like a bruise from the rocks.' The policeman spoke slowly, as if thinking aloud. 'She was a strong woman, a former nurse, trained to lift people. He was not a big man. She injected him with insulin when he was already unconscious. Then, when it was night, she pulled him to the edge of the cliff and — pooh — he is gone.' Manolakis made an expressive gesture with his thin, well-shaped hands.

'Something like that, I suppose,' said Patrick. 'You'd read this, hadn't you, before you came over to Athens?' He pointed to the remark scratched on the wall. Felix must have come round for a few minutes, long enough to pick up a small stone and scrape this attempt to leave a message.

'I know all what is written here,' said Manolakis gravely. 'I know what is new, and what is not.' He paused. 'We have found a small *valitsa* — valise — in the sea. A big stone was inside, to make it stay hidden.'

Patrick was silent.

'You are clever,' he said at last. '*Poli kala.*'

Manolakis beamed.

'You stay with us now, while you finish your holiday,' he said. 'Please. We like very much. We teach you Greek,' he added.

Why not, after all? Manolakis might be hurt if he refused. And besides, there was the sister.

THE END

THE JOFFE BOOKS STORY

We began in 2014 when Jasper agreed to publish his mum's much-rejected romance novel and it became a bestseller.

Since then we've grown into the largest independent publisher in the UK. We're extremely proud to publish some of the very best writers in the world, including Joy Ellis, Faith Martin, Caro Ramsay, Helen Forrester, Simon Brett and Robert Goddard. Everyone at Joffe Books loves reading and we never forget that it all begins with the magic of an author telling a story.

We are proud to publish talented first-time authors, as well as established writers whose books we love introducing to a new generation of readers.

We won Trade Publisher of the Year at the Independent Publishing Awards in 2023 and Best Publisher Award in 2024 at the People's Book Prize. We have been shortlisted for Independent Publisher of the Year at the British Book Awards for the last five years, and were shortlisted for the Diversity and Inclusivity Award at the 2022 Independent Publishing Awards. In 2023 we were shortlisted for Publisher of the Year at the RNA Industry Awards, and in 2024 we were shortlisted at the CWA Daggers for the Best Crime and Mystery Publisher.

We built this company with your help, and we love to hear from you, so please email us about absolutely anything bookish at feedback@joffebooks.com.

If you want to receive free books every Friday and hear about all our new releases, join our mailing list here: www.joffebooks.com/freebooks.

And when you tell your friends about us, just remember: it's pronounced Joffe as in coffee or toffee!